MAR - - 2021

Nations in the News

SAUDI ARABIA

Afghanistan

China

India

Iran

The Koreas

Mexico

Russia

Saudi Arabia

Syria

United Kingdom

Nations in the News
SAUDI ARABIA

BY Norm Geddis

MASON CREST
Philadelphia · Miami

Mason Crest
450 Parkway Drive, Suite D
Broomall, PA 19008
(866) MCP-BOOK (toll free)
www.masoncrest.com

Printed in the United States of America.

First printing
9 8 7 6 5 4 3 2 1

Series ISBN: 978-1-4222-4242-1
Hardcover ISBN: 978-1-4222-4250-6
ebook ISBN: 978-1-4222-7578-8

Cataloging-in-Publication Data is available on file
at the Library of Congress.

Developed and Produced by Print Matters Productions, Inc.
(www.printmattersinc.com)

Cover and Interior Design by Tom Carling, Carling Design Inc.

Contents

Introduction 6

1 Security Issues 18

2 Government and Politics 34

3 Economy 52

4 Quality of Life 66

5 Society and Culture................................. 84

Series Glossary of Key Terms 100

Chronology of Key Events 105

Further Reading & Internet Resources 107

Index 108

Author's Biography... 111

Credits 112

KEY ICONS TO LOOK FOR

Words to Understand: These words with their easy-to-understand definitions will increase the reader's understanding of the text while building vocabulary skills.

Sidebars: This boxed material within the main text allows readers to build knowledge, gain insights, explore possibilities, and broaden their perspectives by weaving together additional information to provide realistic and holistic perspectives.

Educational Videos: Readers can view videos by scanning our QR codes, providing them with additional educational content to supplement the text.

Text-Dependent Questions: These questions send the reader back to the text for more careful attention to the evidence presented there.

Research Projects: Readers are pointed toward areas of further inquiry connected to each chapter. Suggestions are provided for projects that encourage deeper research and analysis.

Series Glossary of Key Terms: This back-of-the-book glossary contains terminology used throughout this series. Words found here increase the reader's ability to read and comprehend higher-level books and articles in this field.

The Masmak fort was used by Abdulaziz bin Abdul Rahman bin Faisal al-Saud (Ibn Saud) as a base to unite the Kingdom of Saudi Arabia and the present-day country. It is now used as a museum, but it is one of the most historic sites in the country.

Saudi Arabia at a Glance

Total Land Area	830,000 square miles
Climate	Harsh, dry desert with great temperature variances
Natural Resources	Petroleum, natural gas, iron ore, gold, copper
Land Use	Agricultural land: 80.7 percent (1.5 percent arable land, 0.1 percent permanent crops, 79.1 percent pasture); forest: 0.5 percent; other: 18.8 percent
Urban Population	83 percent of total population (2018)
Major Urban Areas	Riyadh (6.907 million); Jeddah (4.433 million); Mecca (1.967 million); Medina (1.43 million); Dammam (1.197 million)
Geography	Middle East, bordering the Persian Gulf and the Red Sea, north of Yemen

Introduction

The Kingdom of Saudi Arabia is an **absolute monarchy** and one of the most powerful states in the Middle East. Saudi Arabia spends more on its military than Russia, which gives it the third-largest military budget the world. The country occupies most of what is known as the Arabian Peninsula, a large landmass

A Saudi Air Force EF-2000 Typhoon F2.

Words to Understand

Absolute monarchy: A form of government led by a single individual, usually called a king or a queen, who has control over all aspects of government and whose authority cannot be challenged.

Cleric: A general term for a religious leader such as a priest or imam.

Depose: The act of removing a head of government through force, intimidation, and/or manipulation.

Edict: A proclamation by a person in authority that functions the same as a law.

Embargo: An official ban on trade.

off the northwest coast of Africa, across the Red Sea. Part of the western edge of the country is on the Persian Gulf. The country shares borders with Yemen and Oman on the south; Qatar, Bahrain, and the United Arab Emirates on the east; and Jordan, Iraq, and Kuwait on the north.

As one of the world's top oil producers, Saudi Arabia exerts considerable influence in world affairs. Saudi Arabia has used its oil wealth to build a thriving economy, albeit one that runs primarily on the country's two vast but ultimately finite resources, oil and natural gas. An oil **embargo** led by Saudi Arabia nearly crippled the U.S. economy in the early 1970s. Saudi diplomats convinced other oil-producing nations to stop selling oil to the United States because of U.S. support for Israel in the 1973 Arab-Israeli War.

Today, Saudi Arabia is a country in transition. Oil deposits in the region will be largely depleted over the next century. Alternatives to petroleum-based fuels for automobiles are making the world less reliant on oil, and that's bad news for the oil industry's future as a whole. The trend toward electric vehicles is expected to lower gasoline consumption in the coming decades. Saudi Arabia hopes to perpetuate its prosperity through the development of economic opportunities like tourism and technology.

The fast pace of economic expansion has required an influx of foreign workers and the rapid education of the country's people. The economic boom began when oil production started ramping up in the 1940s. Many Saudi families have transitioned from living in nomadic tribes to the world of educated professionals in about three generations. Someone who is an established Saudi engineer likely has a grandfather who knew only a life of desert wandering.

The House of Saud has ruled the kingdom since its founding in 1930. In reality, the family has ruled some portion of the peninsula, at least part of the time, since 1744. The family rose to power, then was **deposed**, and then returned to power numerous times during the nineteenth century. When the Saudi royal family came to power, it did so with the help of the founders of an ultra-conservative form of Islam called Wahhabism. Wahhabism began in the seventeenth century and advocates for what its adherents consider a pure form of Sunni Islam, one of the two major branches of Islam. (The other major branch is known as Shi'a Islam. The differences between the

In 1973, Saudi Arabia withheld oil from the United State due to U.S. support for Israel in the Arab-Israeli War. This led to gas rationing, long lines at gas stations, and specific schedules for when vehicles could access gas.

Al-Ula is one of the most interesting tourist attractions in Saudi Arabia. Pictured here is a single tomb carved into the side of a dome.

The United States has shared a relationship with Saudi Arabia for many generations. Pictured here, President Franklin Roosevelt sits with Muhammad bin Saud, the first monarch and founder of Saudi Arabia.

two stem from a disagreement over who was the rightful successor to the Prophet Muhammad.)

The main thrust of Wahhabism has been to purge all outside influences from Islam and protect it from new ones, like pop culture. Wahhabism has strict rules and expectations for women. These rules include separating women and men in public and private spaces, as well as the famous burqa requirement for women. A burqa is a body covering that shows only the eyes. In some areas where it is considered inappropriate for women to show their eyes, they must wear a full veil, too.

Time line of women's rights in Saudi Arabia.

Other rules have included prohibitions on women voting, driving, working, teaching, getting an education, being in the same room as men who are not their relatives, and being in public without a male escort. Many of these bans are being lifted, albeit slowly, with incremental changes. For example, women are allowed to go to college, but they must be separated from men. They attend class in a separate room where they watch their professors on a video feed. Today 60 percent of Saudi university students are women.

The recent lifting of the women's driving ban got international attention, because Saudi Arabia was the only country in the world with this type of ban. Videos of women driving went viral after the ban was lifted, including a video of a very happy young lady rapping about being able to drive.

Women are not the only ones affected by Saudi Arabia's strict forms of governance. Men have dress requirements, too. Some Wahhabi **clerics** forbid watching or playing soccer, which is as popular in Saudi Arabia as it is around the world.

A Saudi woman test-drives her new vehicle after being given the right to get a license.

The Wahhabism and the Saudi family dynasty remain a partnership focused on keeping Saudi citizens "pure" and the royal family in power. To that end, Wahhabi police patrol the cities and rural areas of Saudi Arabia, looking for people who are not living according to proper religious **edicts**. Such policing tactics have given the international press some interesting stories to report, like the one about the man who was arrested for eating breakfast with a woman he wasn't related to. Religious clerics and scholars also have political power in Saudi Arabia.

Both internal and external influences have resulted in a slow decline of the power and influence of the religious police. However, many conservative elements in the kingdom, including members of the royal family, fully support a strong religious authority in the country even at the expense of changes that could benefit Saudi Arabia's economy in the long run. These changes would include liberalization of dress codes and alcohol prohibitions and loosening restrictions on how men and women may socialize, work, and participate in education.

IN THE NEWS

Social Media Exposes Sexual Harassment during the Hajj

A #MeToo type movement hit Saudi Arabia in 2018. A single social media post began a flood of similar stories from women who had been grabbed, groped, and worse while performing *tawaf* during their Islamic pilgrimages to Mecca. This pilgrimage is called the Hajj, and all Muslims are expected to make it at least once in their lifetime.

The *tawaf* ritual is, in part, the act of circling the Kaaba, the huge black stone at the center of the Great Mosque, by moving seven times around it counterclockwise. Muhammad commanded his followers to visit Mecca at least once in their lives, if possible, to perform *tawaf*. A Pakistani woman named Sabica Khan began the social movement when she wrote about her experience of having hands on her buttocks and objects poking her backside while circling the Kaaba. The momentum of the crowd prevented her from turning around for fear of falling and being trampled (2,000 trampling deaths occurred during the 2015 Hajj). Thousands of similar reports of groping hit social media like a storm.

Most of the social changes that Saudi Arabia has experienced over the last decade have been because of modernization efforts begun by the country's former king. Plus, the country has a prominent crown prince, Mohammed bin Salman, or MbS for short. His father, King Salman, has granted his son authority over security and economic development, making him one of the country's most powerful leaders.

Mohammed bin Salman's actions as crown prince have shown him to be a brutal leader who tolerates no dissent. Activists have been jailed even after the government has met their demands. Several government officials, even relatives of the crown prince, have been killed or disappeared by Saudi security forces.

The death of Saudi opposition journalist Jamal Khashoggi in October 2018, apparently murdered by Saudi security officials, displays the crown prince as either someone who operates outside both Saudi and international law, or as a leader who does not have control

Protests erupted around the world calling for justice after the death of Saudi journalist Jamal Khashoggi. The United States vowed to end the Saudi-backed war in Yemen weeks after news broke about the Crown Prince's involvement in the murder.

over his own security forces. Khashoggi died at a Saudi consulate in Turkey while being questioned by Saudi security officials. Whether or not the exact truth about Khashoggi's death gets told, the story so far is that several security officials known to be close to Mohammed bin Salman were the ones interacting with him when he died.

The crown prince has initiated a crackdown on corruption that appears to be meant to scare both his own government officials and political opponents. Critics say he has been brutal in his efforts and indifferent to the opposition he is stirring by arresting so many government officials, many of them his relatives. The government is seeking the death penalty for several popular religious clerics caught up in the crackdown. The prince appears to be someone who is trying to squelch opposition rather than effectively deal with corruption.

MbS is staking Saudi Arabia's future on building an international, state-of-the-art tech, construction, and tourism infrastructure. To attract the investment and talent that the country requires, the cities that house this infrastructure will need to be able to accommodate people from all different cultures, just like any metropolitan city. This plan would contradict the stance of the Wahhabis, whose ideology calls for purging Saudi land of all foreign influences.

Pilgrims hold the step in front of the golden door while praying and asking for God's forgiveness in Mecca.

Grand Mosque Seizure

In 1979, 500 followers of an obscure cleric stormed the Grand Mosque in Mecca, Islam's holiest site, taking control of the vast complex. Early evening prayers had just begun, with 50,000 people in attendance. Several dozen attendees, along with most of the and the imams, were taken hostage. The cleric's followers believed he was a prophesied figure in Islamic religion called the Twelfth Imam. The seizure was ended by a joint task force of Saudi Arabian, Pakistani, and French soldiers. France contributed special forces soldiers who were the first into the mosque. The battle returned control of the mosque to Saudi religious authorities.

When people find a better income and more convenient life, they are apt to be willing to change their ways. When people find corrupted, stalled development projects and stagnation, they are likely to seek refuge in tradition. Whether Saudi Arabia will move toward a compromise with international customs or maintain itself as a semi-forbidden kingdom will depend on the successes or failures of economic-development projects and long-term social changes.

Text-Dependent Questions

1. When did the Saudi family first control part of the Arabian Peninsula?
2. True or false: Saudi Arabia spends more on its military than Russia.
3. How does Mohammed bin Salman's plan to modernize Saudi Arabia contradict the stance of the Wahhabis?

Research Project

The current crown prince is not the first one under the current king. Research the crown prince before Mohammed bin Salman and why he lost his office and titles. Describe the circumstances in a narrative report.

Saudi Arabia in the News in the 21st Century

Khashoggi Death: Saudi Arabia Says Journalist Was Murdered
BBC News, October 22, 2018

Saudi Arabia Struck Gold with Corruption Crackdown
Bloomberg Businessweek, January 24, 2018

Saudi Arabia's Crown Prince Promises to Lead His Country "Back to Moderate Islam"
The Telegraph, October 24, 2017

The $2 Trillion Project to Get Saudi Arabia's Economy off Oil
Bloomberg Businessweek, April 21, 2016

No More New Cars or Furniture, Says King as Oil Slump Forces Cuts on Saudi Arabia
The Guardian, October 8, 2015

How U.S. Weapons Will Play a Huge Role in Saudi Arabia's War in Yemen
Washington Post, March 26, 2015

Saudi Arabia's "Reformer" King Abdullah Dies
CNN, January 23, 2015

Saudi Arabia Rejects UN Security Council Seat in Protest Move
New York Times, October 18, 2013

Saudi Arabia Builds Giant Yemen Border Fence
BBC News, April 9, 2013

Saudi Arabia Expels Thousands of Yemeni Workers
The Guardian, April 2, 2013

CHAPTER 1

Security Issues

Saudi Arabia seeks to make itself a dominant power in Middle Eastern affairs, and at times uses its influence on the wider global stage. The country ranks fifth in the world in military spending. Being a Sunni-dominated nation founded on a politically powerful religious movement puts Saudi Arabia in direct opposition to its Shi'a counterpart in Iran. Iran is also a religiously dominated country, but its citizens are primarily adherents of Shi'a Islam. The conflict between these two branches of Islam has created mistrust and generated war since the death of Islam's founder, the prophet Muhammad.

Saudi Arabia has a Shi'a minority concentrated in the Persian Gulf coastal area of the country. Leaders of the Shi'a community have been accused of accepting money and other help from Iran for terrorist attacks within Saudi Arabia. Although it's true that Shi'a extremists have been responsible for some of the ugliest attacks to occur within the country, charges against some religious figures have been based on flimsy evidence when measured against internationally recognized standards of justice.

Words to Understand

Heretical: When someone's beliefs contradict an orthodox religion.

Houthi movement: A Shi'a sect that emerged in Yemen in the 1990s in opposition to the Sunni-led government. The assassination of its leader began the current hostilities in the Saudi-Yemeni conflict.

Sortie: A defensive attack on the battlefield.

Much of Saudi Arabia's money is spent on its military forces.

Saudi Arabia's Security Issues at a Glance

Military Size	251,500 total personnel
Military Service	17 years of age for voluntary service; no conscription
Military Branches	Ministry of Defense: Royal Saudi Land Forces, Royal Saudi Naval Forces (includes Marine Forces and Special Forces), Royal Saudi Air Force (Al-Quwwat al-Jawwiya al-Malakiya as-Sa'udiya), Royal Saudi Air Defense Forces, Royal Saudi Strategic Rocket Forces, Ministry of the National Guard (SANG)
Military Spending	$69.5 billion USD (2017); 9.85 percent of GDP (2016)
Terrorist Groups (foreign-based)	al-Qaeda, Islamic State of Iraq and al-Sham (ISIS)
Illicit Drugs	Regularly enforces the death penalty for drug traffickers, with foreigners being convicted and executed disproportionately

Shi'a community members pray inside a mosque.

Though Saudi Arabia has been a reliable ally of the United States, a religiously conservative portion of Saudi society leans more toward a type of Islamic extremism that sees the United States as, more or less, a force of evil in the world. Today Saudi Arabia's biggest security challenge may be how to reconcile the country's urge to modernize with its dedication to a rigid way of life.

Clerics who have persistently demonized the United States are, at least in part, responsible for radicalizing a number of the people who carried out the September 11th terrorist attacks in the United States. The majority of individuals involved in carrying out the attacks were Saudi citizens.

The Saudi government takes criticism from the United States seriously, and it strives to promote a positive image of the country to the American public. What the United States, Europe, and the rest of the world think of Saudi Arabia matters, so when several court cases about the country's culpability in the September 11th terrorist attacks caused American opinion of the country to take a downward turn, the country stepped up arrests of religious clerics who preached violence against the United States or other countries.

Fifteen of the 19 hijackers involved in the September 11th attacks were citizens of Saudi Arabia.

Conflicts

Saudi Arabia has military, ideological, and religious conflicts with other nations in its region. The country is often taken to task for its human rights abuses by various governments and organizations. Canada got into a diplomatic skirmish with Saudi Arabia over human rights abuses in 2018. Specifically, Canada was critical of the arrest of peaceful activists who had advocated for a woman's right to drive. This resulted in Saudi Arabia pulling students from Canada and freezing all trade.

Regionally, Saudi Arabia's biggest nemesis is Iran. The two countries are at odds with each other in a power struggle over who gets to dominate the Middle East. Religious differences make the conflict between the two nations more intense. Each country follows a different branch of Islam. Saudi Arabia is a nation of Sunni Muslims. Iran has a large majority of Shi'a Muslims, at around 90 percent of the country's total population. The Sunni and Shi'a sects of Islam forked shortly after the founding of Islam. Each sect believes the other is **heretical**.

Saudi-Yemeni Conflict

Saudi Arabia has the third-largest defense budget in the world behind the United States and China. Although Saudi Arabia never has claimed outwardly expansionist aims for its territory, the country has recently become involved in a civil war in Yemen.

In the 1990s, a religious and political movement began in northern Yemen near the border of Saudi Arabia. The movement has become known as the **Houthi movement**, and its adherents are known as Houthis. The Shi'a background of the Houthi sect puts them in opposition to Sunni Islam, which is the basis of Saudi Arabia's Wahhabism. The Houthis have received the majority of their financial support from Iran.

The Houthis have blamed Saudi Arabia for fostering corruption in their Sunni-led Yemeni government. From 2015 on, the Houthis have been calling their leaders an illegitimate puppet government controlled by Saudi Arabia and the United States. Hostilities began when Houthi rebel troops shelled the Saudi Arabian border city of Najran. Border skirmishes between 2016 and 2018 left Najran partially occupied by Houthi rebels. As of

A group of Houthis protest Saudi-led air strikes.

early 2018, Houthis controlled about a 100-mile stretch of Saudi Arabia, from Najran to Jizan.

The Saudis have launched a number of attacks against the Iran-supported Houthi tribes. The attacks have been criticized for their indifference toward collateral damage, which means the unintentional killing of civilians and/or the destruction of non-militarized properties.

The organization Human Rights Watch has accused Saudi Arabia of war crimes and, by implication, the United States as well. Saudi Arabia has launched several air strikes against civilian targets, including one that hit a refugee camp, destroying its hospital and market. It has also brought massive troop deployments into civilian areas and repressed peaceful protests and media coverage. Human Rights Watch has asserted, "The United States may have become a party to the conflict, creating obligations under the laws of war." The United States has provided arms, intelligence, and logistical services to Saudi Arabia throughout the conflict.

Alliances

Saudi Arabia is officially a nonaligned country. This means that it does not align itself directly with any power bloc. The Non-Aligned Movement sprang up during the Cold War between the United States

After news broke of air strikes in Yemen, backed by the United States and United Kingdom, protests erupted in cities like London.

Saudi Arabia's crackdown on religious clerics.

and Soviet Union (Russia) in the 1960s. Nations in the movement stayed out of U.S.-Soviet conflicts. Today the term still tends to reflect an avoidance of the conflicts between the United States and Russia, but China is also a major world player now with its own ambitions to further the nonaligned cause.

Although Saudi Arabia does not align itself with any bloc, two of its biggest trading partners are the United States and China. The

country has a warmer relationship with these two countries than it does with Russia.

Regional Relations

Saudi Arabia dominates Sunni culture in the Middle East. It has strong alliances with Pakistan and the United Arab Emirates. A complicated relationship with Egypt has given rise to periods of strong cooperation and periods of discord. Relations during the 2010s have been strained over differing approaches to the Syrian civil war—a conflict involving the government of Syria and various anti-government forces that has created one of the worst humanitarian disasters in history—and the conflict in Yemen.

Iran stands as Saudi Arabia's biggest adversary. One of the reasons for the world's extreme apprehension about Iran having a nuclear bomb is that Saudi Arabia would feel compelled to begin a regional cold war by acquiring a weapon similar in destructive scope.

Academics who study Middle Eastern culture and conflicts have speculated that Saudi Arabia may already have an understanding with Pakistan, a nuclear power itself. Pakistan armed itself with a nuclear weapon in response to its own adversary, India. Pakistan may be willing to supply one or two of these weapons to its ally, Saudi Arabia, if Iran gets a nuclear weapon first.

International Relations

Saudi Arabia is a founding member of many international organizations like the United Nations and the Organization of the Petroleum Exporting Countries (OPEC). The country has a strong relationship with both the United States and Europe and is seeking to build a similarly warm relationship with China. Saudi Arabia focuses its attention on Middle Eastern affairs and generally does not assert itself on a wider scale, except as issues relate to regional conflicts, such as the 1973 oil embargo over the Arab-Israeli War. Israel gets scorned publicly by Saudi clerics and the government, but behind the scenes both countries cooperate on mutual problems with Iran.

Saudi Arabia has accused Qatar of supporting terrorism. Qatar is a country occupying the smaller peninsula jutting out from the main Arabian Peninsula into the Persian Gulf. Even though Qatar contributed 1,000 troops to the Saudi-backed offensive in Yemen in 2015, Saudi Arabia cut all diplomatic ties with Qatar in June of 2017. According to Saudi accusations, Qatar has given money to ISIS, al-Qaeda, and the Muslim Brotherhood, all while hosting

In 2015, Qatar sent 1,000 troops to assist with the war in Yemen.

the largest U.S. military base in the Middle East. Qatar has sought better relations with Iran, which Saudi Arabia sees as a threat. After discovering Qatar had purchased Russian air defense missiles, the crown prince sought to invade Qatar during the summer of 2018 but could not get President Trump's blessing. The crown prince even suggested scooping a moat out of the desert and turning Qatar into an island.

The United States is in an awkward position in Qatar. The Qatari government denies many of the accusations leveled against it. Qatar denies sending support to ISIS but does admit to sending support to al-Qaeda–related forces fighting in Syria. Saudi Arabia did the same. Any military action in the small country would threaten the U.S. military base and command and control center there, and an invasion by Saudi Arabia could bring Iran into the conflict.

Human Trafficking

The U.S. Department of State classified Saudi Arabia as a Tier 2 Watch List country in its international human trafficking report for 2017. These are countries that do not meet the state department's

Women and children are most susceptible to human trafficking.

minimum standards for the prevention and prosecution of human trafficking crimes but are making efforts to do so. Saudi Arabia has been warned by the United States that it must form a strategy for reducing instances of abuse among the more than 10 million foreign workers in the country.

Women from the Philippines and other Southeast Asian nations come to Saudi Arabia as domestic workers. The Saudi government provides no protections against the mistreatment of foreign women working in homes. Typical reports of abuse include wage theft, the taking and withholding of travel documents, sexual harassment, and beatings.

No mechanism exists for charging Saudi citizens with crimes when foreign workers make complaints. In fact, the complaint usually results in the worker being fired. The employer often keeps the travel documents as a punishment. The worker is then unable to return home and likely joins the tens of thousands of homeless ex–foreign workers trying to exist without proper documentation. The Saudi government has set up shelters for workers who were fired and cannot return home.

Saudi Diplomats Accused of Trafficking Humans into the United States

Dozens of Saudi diplomats have been accused of underpaying and abusing their household staff. The workers usually come from poverty-stricken and war-torn countries in Africa and Asia. The conditions they find with their new employers look like little more than slavery. Accusations in 35 lawsuits filed since 2000, along with an investigation by the U.S. Government Accountability Office, show instances of physical abuse, the withholding of travel documents, sexual abuse, and denial of wages. One victim reported that her passport and visa were taken from her. She was locked inside of a house, paid about 50 cents an hour, and told that if she went outside, "Americans" would attack her.

Illicit Drugs

Saudi Arabia beats out just about every other nation in the harsh-drug-law category. Death seems to be the preferred punishment for everything from possession to trafficking. The weight of these strident laws falls mainly on foreign workers. Saudi citizens are rarely executed for drug crimes such as simple possession. But a handful of foreign workers have been executed for low-level drug crimes such as possession or trafficking in small amounts. Even in the United States, where drug penalties are considered harsh, the low-level crimes that result in hangings in Saudi Arabia would be no more than misdemeanors.

Military

The Saudi military has just over 250,000 total military personnel, according to the International Institute for Strategic Studies. The total budget for all branches is $69.5 billion, which makes it the third most expensive military in the world. The United States and

Deera Square is a public space in Saudi Arabia in which public executions—usually beheadings—take place.

Saudi Arabian National Guardsmen learn about the M252 from a member of the U.S. 1st Battalion, 325th Airborne Infantry.

China spend more on their militaries than Saudi Arabia, whereas Russia spends a little bit less.

The large Saudi military exists mainly as a deterrent to Iranian aggression. Iran has more than twice as many citizens as Saudi Arabia and has shown a willingness to throw untrained civilians onto the battlefield with little in the way of weapons and support.

The last major Saudi military action was its participation in the Gulf War. When Iraq invaded Kuwait in 1990, the United States led a coalition of countries to push Iraqi forces out of Kuwait. Saudi Arabia hosted the coalition countries and participated in the 800,000-troop invasion of Iraq. Its air force flew 7,000 **sorties** over Iraq.

Terrorist Groups

Prior to the mid-1990s, terrorist incidents were rare, though some of the attacks that did occur impacted the kingdom in a big way. After the first Gulf War, U.S. military bases were established in Saudi Arabia. Extremists turned the presence of non-Muslims into a rallying cry. Terrorist attacks began to happen with greater frequency after 1995.

Civilians and military forces celebrate as Iraqi forces retreat from Kuwait.

The rise of the Ayatollah Khomeini in Iran inspired a fanatical group, Ikhwan, in Saudi Arabia to seize Islam's most holy site, the Grand Mosque, in 1979. The group was not directly tied to the ayatollah. In contrast, they thought their own leader was the redeemer predicted in the Qu'ran, called the Mahdi, or Twelfth Imam. The group believed that taking the mosque would help start their own revolution inside Saudi Arabia.

The group was led by a powerful Saudi family, a member of which had once been the Grand Mufti of Saudi Arabia—the country's highest religious and legal figure. One of the members of the family, Mohammed Abdullah al-Qahtani, was believed to be the Mahdi. Worshippers who were taken hostage inside the Grand Mosque said that al-Qahtani had some of the physical features that the Qu'ran and Islamic tradition attribute to the Mahdi.

For two weeks in 1979, terrorists occupied the Grand Mosque.

The terrorists held the mosque for two weeks. Only after a counterattack by Saudi, Pakistani, and French forces was the mosque recaptured at a cost of over 100 deaths on each side. Of the remaining 68 terrorists captured alive, the Saudi government executed all but two. Nothing like the Grand Mosque seizure has happened since, though a plot to undertake a similar attack was foiled in its planning stages in 2017.

Text-Dependent Questions

1. True or False: Religious differences are partly responsible for the conflict in Yemen.

2. What is the rank of the Saudi military by expenditure?

3. In Saudi Arabia, most drug crimes are punishable by what penalty?

Research Project

Several factors have led Saudi Arabia to spend money on a large military. Research some of these factors, including strained relations with other countries, the desire to maintain influence, and civil unrest and terrorist activity within Saudi Arabia. Make a list of five factors that explain why the country feels a large military is in its interest. Include how each factor impacts Saudi society.

Government and Politics

Saudi Arabia is one of the world's few remaining absolute monarchies. King Salman, the current monarch, has the power to make decrees that carry the weight of law, negate any law previously passed by the country's legislature, or veto any law the legislature does pass. The Consultative Assembly is Saudi Arabia's legislature, roughly equivalent to the U.S. Congress or British Parliament, except the king can toss out or tweak anything it does on a whim. The king also appoints all of the members of the assembly.

However, in reality, the king delegates much of his power. He has a prime minister and other officials who manage the day-to-day affairs of passing laws. Many of those officials are members of the ruling Saudi royal family. They tend to know what the king wants and carry out his will. There is little in the way of political opposition

Words to Understand

Constitution: A written document or unwritten set of traditions that outline the powers, responsibilities, and limitations of a government.

Idolatry: The worship of an image or representation of a god.

Municipal elections: Elections held for office on the local level, such as town, city, or county.

Recourse: The legal right, and the system that enforces that right, to seek compensation from another who has done one harm.

Totalitarian: A form of government where power is in the hands of a single person or group.

King Salman (*right*) shakes hands with U.S. Secretary of State John Kerry upon his arrival at Andrews Air Force Base.

Saudi Arabia's Government and Legal System at a Glance

Independence	September 23, 1932
National Holiday	Saudi National Day (anniversary of the unification of the kingdom), September 23rd
National Symbol(s)	Palm tree
Constitution	Basic law of government issued by royal decree, March 1, 1992
Legal System	Sharia (Islamic) legal system, with elements of Egyptian, French, and customary law
Voting Eligibility	18 years of age; male only except for municipal elections

in Saudi Arabia. Although no law exists banning opposition to the king's government, the religious police usually find a moral crime to use against a figure who may be able to challenge the king politically.

Far from a democracy, Saudi Arabia is also something other than a **totalitarian** state, even though some of the official state policies are considered by other countries and various human rights groups to be totalitarian. Much of the power responsible for carrying out more oppressive policies, like those regarding the behavior of women and the punishment of criminals, is held by the religious police.

Religion exists side by side with the government in Saudi Arabia. The religious authorities make their own laws and determine their own punishments when it comes to moral crimes. One can break the moral laws of Saudi Arabia simply by choosing to dine with the wrong person.

However, the power of the religious police is waning as Saudi Arabia seeks to improve its position in world affairs by opening up its economy to foreign investment. This means more outsiders in Saudi Arabia's urban areas—more Christians, Hindus, and others who may be atheist, Buddhist, Taoist, or Confucian. The Saudi royal family is seeking to compromise with the creed of the religious authorities who do not want people of other religions on their land, and certainly not with the right to practice their customs. This has meant many recent changes to the legal nature of doing business in Saudi Arabia.

Some aspects of the Saudi system still make life difficult for outsiders, but many changes in the way government operates have given more people, both Saudis and outsiders, greater **recourse** to government protection and help. A long road remains before all aspects of the Saudi government are up to the Western standards—though that ever happening seems unlikely. Saudi Arabia doesn't want to be "Western." The future looks more like a balancing act, with Saudi society tolerating some Western, Asian, and other cultures who, in turn, will be tolerating the local customs they find cumbersome.

Government Type

Absolute monarchies are pretty easy to understand on the surface. One man rules everything by qualification of his birth. Women can rule, too, in some monarchies but not in Saudi Arabia. Only male descendants of the first king can sit the throne.

The Masmak Fortress stands as a museum and includes photos of the royal Saud family throughout.

The reality is a little more complicated. Saudi Arabia has a vast empire with a rich culture. The king can't do everything, so he delegates responsibility. The Saudi government is a vast network of bureaucracies, all of them run by members of the king's family. Each was formed and given authority by the king's decree. Recently, the king named a new crown prince, and he has been given authority over corruption, government reform, foreign investment, and economic development. He is currently the most powerful man in Saudi Arabia after the king and seems to be very active in seeking reform. Still, absolute power remains with King Salman, and though he has delegated significant powers to the crown prince, he can take them away at any time.

Mohammed bin Salman

Young and attractive, Mohammed bin Salman brings a new image to the Saudi royal family, an image once dominated by elderly figures in positions of power and young royals on a quest for the world's best retail shopping. The country's new crown prince projects an

Crown Prince Mohammad bin Salman.

image that is part entrepreneur, part activist, and part hipster. In his most effective media images, he looks like the kind of guy who is about to share a really great playlist. He is known throughout the kingdom by his nickname, MbS.

But behind a carefully tailored public persona are some deeds that have brought criticism from human rights groups and other governments. The prince initiated a crackdown on government corruption by arresting over 100 government officials, many of them members of the Saud royal family, and keeping them detained in a luxurious hotel. The suspects were held in the Ritz-Carlton in Riyadh from November 2017 until January 2018. One of those arrested, the crown prince's youngest uncle, has not been seen in public since. (The Saudi government denies rumors that he was killed in a shootout with police.) Along with the detainees at the Ritz, 400 more suspects were rounded up later.

The accused in the hotel and other suspects have faced a choice: subjecting themselves to a legal system that makes up many of its rules as it goes along, or paying their way out of their legal troubles. One Saudi billionaire paid $1 billion for his freedom. The payments are said to be recompense for corruption. Many Saudis in the billionaire class see it as a shakedown by the crown prince for their money and power.

While the hotel detention was going on, many wealthy Saudis left the country, their status somewhat insulted by the fact they had to leave via "public transportation," because the crown prince had

Saudi Arabia's most elite "prison," the Ritz-Carlton, held over 100 government officials suspected of corruption.

grounded all private jets during the crackdown. The wealthy who went into exile did so in first-class style but on commercial airlines.

By the standards usually afforded to Saudi royals, the prince's crackdown has been brutal. This has created a backlash against him and his plans for reform. However, from the prince's point of view, he has responsibilities that go to the heart of the nature of government and power. A monarchy is a form of government that, perhaps accidentally, invites internal power struggles. Monarchies tend to base their claim to power on a pact with God, and Saudi Arabia is no different. But a belief in a benevolent deity authorizing a government's authority doesn't prevent the ugliest human instincts from dominating officials with that authority.

The prince is seeking the execution of 10 of the men arrested in his crackdown, and that is just the beginning. Those under threat of the death penalty are mostly religious clerics. This has put MbS in the position of trying to modernize a country with some of the most barbaric techniques of gaining power and forcing change. Actions like this can create deep resentments that last for decades and foster ongoing violence—a long way from the prince's goal of creating a society with cool places to work and fun places to hang out.

The Road Ahead

By Saudi Arabia's own estimate, proven oil reserves will run out in 90 years. Proven reserves are those areas where the oil in the ground has been measured and quantified with the best science and technology available. However, those estimates may be unreliable. Critics of the Saudi calculations say the reserves may be much lower. They point out flaws in Saudi reports, such as using certain data from the 1980s without accounting for depletion between then and now. The Saudi calculations may be off by as much as 40 percent.

Loss of petroleum production means the loss of the single most important sector of the Saudi economy. MbS will want to be king of a prosperous Saudi Arabia, not a decaying one. To that end, he may feel the need to consolidate power now. His economic plans include building up the construction, technology, and tourism sectors. Each of these sectors will require social changes in the kingdom so that Saudis can compete with the rest of the world.

Justice for Sheikh Nimr

EXECUTED BY
SAUDI REGIME
ON 2ND JAN 2016
FOR DEMANDING
HUMAN RIGHTS
FOR ALL CITIZENS

WWW.IHRC.ORG
WWW.INMINDS.COM

Actions by the House of Saud have been widely criticized and protested around the world. In 2016, the execution of Sheikh Nimr was condemned by multiple countries. Nimr was critical of the Saudi government and was eventually arrested and put to death for disobeying the country's rulers.

Tourism will struggle to attract travelers from Africa, Asia, Europe, and the Americas without the country making some accommodations for alcohol use. As with most Arab nations, alcohol is forbidden in every circumstance. Other nations with Islamic governments allow alcohol to be sold and consumed in certain areas. The religious authorities, with power of their own separate from the king, will need to be convinced to permit any social change that moves the country more toward the non-Islamic world.

Saudi Arabia has developed a plan, called Saudi Vision 2030, to diversify its economy by expanding its non-petroleum-based sectors. Infrastructure technology, education, medicine, and tourism are seen as the future economic pillars of Saudi Arabia. The plan calls for the development of construction technology that not only can be applied to Saudi infrastructure like roads, sewers, and buildings but exported to benefit other countries' infrastructures as well. Saudi leaders hope these technology exports will offset the expected decline of petroleum exports.

The official logo for Saudi Vision 2030.

The Political Rights of Women

Though an absolute monarchy, Saudi Arabia's royal family has allowed for **municipal elections** since the 1920s, before the formation of Saudi Arabia. The elections have happened irregularly and were cancelled entirely for most of the reign of King Faisal, who ruled from 1964 through 1975. Elections were again postponed in 2009 to consider allowing women the vote. Issues surrounding women's suffrage were the need of an ID card (which most women didn't have at the time), segregated polling stations for women, the hiring of female poll workers, and security of female voters against attack by extremists. In 2012 King Abdullah decreed that in forthcoming elections women would be allowed to vote and run for office. The 2015 municipal elections saw 17 women elected to public office throughout Saudi Arabia.

Constitution

The treaty that created the Kingdom of Saudi Arabia names the Qu'ran as the **constitution** of the kingdom. What that means has been open to interpretation. It would seem that the king is the ultimate arbitrator of all governmental issues. But with religious law intertwining within governmental policy, the boundaries of the authority of the state are unclear. One effect of this confusion is that arrests require less rigid scrutiny than those in the West, where the law requires probable cause and tools like warrants are needed before searches are conducted and arrests made. In keeping with the influence of religion in public life, all judges in the country are also religious scholars.

Saudi National Day

Saudi National Day didn't become an official national holiday until 2015, though it has been celebrated as a holiday since the founding of the kingdom. On September 23, 1932, King Ibn Saud signed a treaty creating the nation of Saudi Arabia, with himself as the first king. Saudi Arabia celebrates the day with local festivals that offer opportunities to participate in the nation's cultural heritage, including traditional dancing and singing under Saudi flags posted all over buildings.

Cyclists celebrate Saudi National Day.

The Funeral of King Abdullah

King Abdullah was the last Saudi king to be a son of Saudi Arabia's first king, Ibn Saud. King Abdullah began Saudi Arabia's current liberalization trend by allowing women to vote, though only in municipal elections. Like all Saudi kings, he received a solemn funeral procession followed by burial in an unmarked grave, as Wahhabism considers emotional displays at a funeral to be akin to **idolatry**. The government initiated no mourning period, shops opened as usual, and only quiet respect was offered by the public attending the procession.

The first king of Saudi Arabia.

Legal System

Saudi Arabia does not have a written constitution, but it does have what is called the "Basic Law of Saudi Arabia." Adopted by royal decree in 1992, the Basic Law outlines the responsibilities of government institutions. It states that the king must obey Sharia law and that the Qu'ran and *Sunna*, the traditional legal customs of Islam, are the basis for the constitution of Saudi Arabia. Interpretation of the Qu'ran and *Sunna* is the responsibility of a group of religious

In Saudi Arabia the Qu'ran is the law.

scholars known as the ulema. Their writings influence the judges who must apply Sharia law in court, which gives them a kind of influence similar to but not as formal as a supreme court.

Criminal Law

Saudi Arabian law is most famous for its punishments: the cutting off of hands for robbery, the cutting off of heads for witchcraft and sorcery, and so forth. Such punishments are part of the criminal landscape. By comparison, Saudi Arabia has about double the number of reported executions as the United States. This does not count unreported executions of suspected terrorists by the country's intelligence services. However, although punishments can be brutal, and nonmilitary executions are carried out in public, beheadings are not the Wednesday-afternoon entertainment that Westerners seem to imagine takes place in every Saudi town square.

Sharia law, as the Saudi legal system interprets it, recognizes three categories of crime. *Huddud* are crimes with fixed punishments found in the Qu'ran or *Sunna*. Punishments for these crimes must be carried out in public. A convict cannot be pardoned by the victim or the state because these crimes, including theft, adultery, drinking alcohol, and leaving the Islamic faith, are seen as crimes against God. Punishments include execution by stoning or beheading, cutting off of limbs, and lashings. Executions may be followed by a crucifixion of the dead body, or just part of it, such as the mounting of a severed head.

Qisas are crimes against a person for which the person or their family can request retaliatory punishment from the court. In short, these are the "eye-for-an-eye" crimes, and even recently there have been reports of surgical removal of eyes as punishment for the loss of an eye to a victim of a car accident.

Murder is a *qisas* crime. Families of murder victims can ask for the death penalty as punishment, or they can ask for a monetary payment from the murderer's family. *Diyya*, as these payments are called, can be requested in any amount. Some of the more exorbitant *diyya* have led government officials and members of the royal family to express interest in putting limits on the amount that can be requested. This is similar to calls for tort reform in the United States, where large sums of money have been sought from corporations, wealthy individuals, and celebrities for various injuries.

The third category of criminal law in Saudi Arabia is *tazir*. These crimes have been established for the purpose of maintaining a fair and smoothly functioning society. The list of offenses includes everything from jaywalking to bribery. Lashings and jail sentences are the typical punishment for *tazir*.

Family Law

Saudi Arabia doesn't have a separate family court system. The general court for a locality will hear cases involving inheritance, divorce, and adoption. Sharia law creates a separate set of rights for men and women within a family. A man can have multiple wives, and Saudi Arabia has been running a campaign against what it calls "spinsterhood" by advocating greater polygamy. Those who can afford an extra wife are encouraged to consider taking a second or third as a good deed for society. Saudi men can have up to four wives, and more with special permission. An imam who started a Twitter hashtag that roughly translates to "marry a second wife if you can" said that men should take more wives because "women expire, unlike men."

Men may divorce their wives immediately and without justification. Unless a husband grants divorce, women must prove harm in court to obtain one on their own. Evidence standards for women require that she bring up to six male witnesses on her behalf to prove abuse. For this reason, women usually do not try to obtain a divorce through the court. After a divorce, a husband is obligated to financially support his wife, or wives, for four months and 10 days. Fathers get automatic custody of sons from seven years old and daughters from nine years old.

Commercial Law

Commercial law in Saudi Arabia runs on two tracks. Technically, commercial law operates under Sharia. Saudi courts have been known to favor Saudis over citizens of other nations, even other Islamic nations. But Sharia law lays out rules for judges when they decide cases. For example, when deciding damages, a judge will take whatever amount would go to someone of the Islamic faith and cut it in half for a Jew or Christian, and to a 16th for someone who follows another religion or is atheist. Also, Sharia courts do not have a concept of things like lost opportunity, which in Western courts allows investors to go after, among other things, fraudulent schemes and not only recoup their investment but also the money they would have made had the scheme been legitimate.

The uneven and uncodified nature of Sharia in Saudi Arabia has made foreign investors, especially non-Muslims, wary of investing in Saudi projects. Wanting to create a revenue stream of outside investment into the country, the royal family decreed the creation of "special tribunals" in 2003 that created an investment "space." Legal scholars were able to rationalize away many of the Sharia rules that made recouping losses due to fraud difficult for investors who did not practice Sunni Islam. However, this space and its special rules that functioned more like a Western legal system were limited to large investments. The result was that there was one type of commercial justice for some Saudis and another for outsiders. Wealthy Saudis still get greater recourse rights on their investments than Saudis who, for example, own small businesses.

Legislature and Political Parties

Though Saudi Arabia has a Consultative Assembly, its powers as a legislature are limited to making suggestions to the king. The members of the assembly are all chosen by the king; only city council seats and other local government offices are filled by elected representatives. Half of the members of the *majlis* (another name for the Consultative Assembly) attended U.S. colleges, and most have doctoral degrees. The membership of the council is chosen by geography in proportion to population size of each province. This is done by tradition and could change if the king wishes. Shi'a representatives from minority provinces declined the last time the king chose new assembly members in 2013 because of a lack of influence and animosity from some Sunni members.

The Consultative Assembly has been gaining power incrementally in recent years. Its meeting chamber in Al Yamamah Palace now has a separate seating section for women. The king appointed 30 female members to the assembly in 2013. As of 2017, women make up 20 percent of the body. Still, the possibility of major reform originating from the assembly is slim. The assembly is made up of members who are already established in their fields; as such, they

Notes on Sharia

Sharia law is not one kind of law any more than the word *sport* represents one kind of game. In general, Sharia law means basing a system of justice on the Qu'ran, plus additional writings on the sayings of Muhammed. These writings are called the *Sunna*. Many of the sayings have to do with how followers should dress and act. Based on a traditional understanding of the text, judges (who are also religious scholars) decide everything from the credibility of witnesses to the type of punishment a convict shall receive.

Sharia law is interpreted many different ways from culture to culture. Often inside the same country, different sects will have their own courts for issues like local crime, family law, and business law. Some interpretations are very literal in nature, whereas others take a more symbolic approach. Literalists feel that if the Qu'ran or *Sunna* spell out specific punishments, they should be followed exactly. Moderate forms of Islam use the texts as a guideline but keep actual punishments in line with contemporary standards. For example, a moderate and a literalist may interpret a saying in the *Sunna* that requires the execution of certain criminals differently. The moderate may interpret it as meaning that the crime should be punished in accordance with what is severe in the current day and age. A literalist will advocate carrying out executions as described in the writings no matter how brutal.

are unlikely to support any kind of major political reform. Today the assembly's influence stems from authority given to it by the monarch for economic-development programs. Members also get to vote on the budgets for numerous government ministries.

The monarchy feels that political parties are an unnecessary distraction, and they are banned in Saudi Arabia. However, this has not stopped several expatriate parties from forming. These are parties formed outside of Saudi Arabia by Saudis who have left the country because of political or other oppression. Any activities that these parties may have inside the country are illegal, and anyone living inside Saudi Arabia who joins one is committing a crime that can result in jail and lashings.

Some of the political parties are the same kind that are found in most countries. A Green Party of Saudi Arabia sprung up in 2001 but appears to have gone inactive around 2009. According to an Egyptian government website, the party, though organized from America, did manage to influence the underground LGBTQ community in Saudi Arabia.

The Movement for Islamic Reform in Arabia, known as MIRA, is a London-based party that seeks the violent overthrow of the monarchy. It wants a pure Sharia society without a monarch. Police arrested over 20 supporters in Jeddah in 2004 for stirring up anti-government sentiment.

The Judicial Branch

The legal system in Saudi Arabia was founded by the first king, King Ibn Saud. Although the system has a structure of courts designated to handle different issues, such as criminal, commercial, and civil, it also has religious and secret courts. What has been missing in the legal system's structure is a written code.

Courts in the United States operate using at least two sets of codes when hearing a case. The first set of codes contain the laws passed by the legislature. The second contains the court's own rules for how things are done. These rules are called the code of procedure. They cover everything from when the courtroom opens to how evidence is to be admitted and handled to prevent tampering.

In the United States and other Western countries, judges have a lot of leeway in how their courtrooms operate, but rules for evidence and other procedural matters are usually uniform and defined by a board of judges at the state level. Until recently, Saudi Arabia had neither written laws nor written rules for the court. A code of procedure that was introduced in 2001 has been ignored in many courts, especially local ones. Each judge gets to make up the rules for evidence, witnesses, and everything else. In Saudi Arabia, if a judge doesn't like the look of a witness, he can prevent the witness from testifying.

As the country has looked for more outside investment, the Saudi government has been pressured by business interests to create a more consistent judicial system by writing down its laws.

The government began creating a written legal code in 2010. The country's justice minister announced an eight-volume set of legal precedents and principles that will guide courts until a more formal legal code can be created.

Text-Dependent Questions

1. What is the term for Saudi Arabia's form of government?

2. Sharia law, as the Saudi legal system interprets it, recognizes what three categories of crime?

3. True or false: Political parties are banned in Saudi Arabia.

Research Project

Sharia law is not one type of legal system but a matrix of similar systems, like Western law. French and American law have distinct differences, such as presumption of innocence, yet both fall under the category of Western law. Research another Islamic country with a Sharia-based legal system, and compare and contrast its judicial practices with those of Saudi Arabia's.

Economy

The Saudi government is determined to guide the country to a future where more than oil powers the economy. The Saudis have more access to more raw power than anywhere on Earth. Solar power would be as natural a fit to Saudi Arabia as oil has been. To that end, the Saudi government is investing in several large solar arrays. It is experimenting with wind power, too—there's often as much wind in the desert as sun. However, harsh sun conditions create engineering issues for wind turbines that haven't been completely overcome.

Desalination of water has been another important part of the Saudi development strategy. Saudi Arabia is surrounded by seawater, yet has few freshwater resources. The Ras Al-Khair Power and Desalination Plant is the world's largest; its technology removes salt from water to make it drinkable. Construction of the plant began in 2011 and was completed in 2014. Water from the plant is piped to Riyadh and its suburbs.

Words to Understand

Central bank: A government-authorized bank whose purpose is to provide money to retail, commercial, investment, and other banks.

Monetary policy: The various economic adjustments, mechanisms, and practices meant to steer a nation's economy in a particular direction.

Subsidy: Money given by a government to a particular industry or business as a form of assistance.

The Saudi currency is known as the riyal.

Saudi Arabia's Economy at a Glance (all figures 2017)

Currency	Riyal, 2017 exchange rate: 3.75 riyals per U.S. dollar
Labor Force	13.8 million, 6.7 percent in agriculture, 21.4 percent in industry, 71.9 percent in services
Per Capita Income (PPP)	$54,500 (2017)
Inflation Rate (consumer prices)	−0.9 percent (2017)
Gross Domestic Product (GDP)	$1.775 trillion
Overall Unemployment	6 percent (2017)
Industries	Crude oil production, petroleum refining, petrochemicals, industrial gases, cement, fertilizer, plastics, metals, commercial ship repair, commercial aircraft repair, construction
Imports	Machinery, foodstuffs, chemicals, motor vehicles, textiles
Import Partners	China 15.4 percent, United States 13.6 percent, United Arab Emirates 6.5 percent, Germany 5.8 percent, Japan 4.1 percent, India 4.1 percent, South Korea 4 percent
Exports	Petroleum and petroleum products
Export Partners	Japan 12.2 percent, China 11.7 percent, South Korea 9 percent, India 8.9 percent, United States 8.3 percent, United Arab Emirates 6.7 percent, Singapore 4.2 percent

Currency and Banking System

The Saudi Arabian Monetary Authority acts as the **central bank** of the nation. The central bank maintains oversight of retail banks, financial institutions, and insurance companies, as well as having the traditional role of setting **monetary policy**.

The Saudi riyal is the country's currency. It has been the official currency since the days when the country was known as the Kingdom of Hejaz. Only coins were available in Saudi Arabia until 1953. The first paper currency was a script issued to Hajj pilgrims that could be exchanged for goods and services in Mecca. Merchants and locals found the paper script more convenient than coinage and started using it for trade, influencing the Saudi money authority to create and issue paper riyals on a wide scale.

Banks have traditionally operated on the Western method of interest banking. The Islamic faith prohibits the charging of interest, which in the negative sense is referred to as usury. Some countries like Iran prohibit Western-style banking and allow only Islamic banking. Islamic banking differs from interest banking in that instead of charging interest on loans over time, a one-time fee is charged up front. For

Pilgrims exchange money near a mosque in Mecca.

example, a customer might get a 10,000-riyal loan with a fee of 1,000 riyals. The customer pays the Islamic bank the fee and pays back the loan over time with no additional interest. A number of established banks are transitioning to or adding the option of Islamic banking.

Labor Force

The social benefits afforded Saudis since the explosion of oil wealth in the 1960s have left a "labor gap." Saudi Arabia imports much of its workforce from the Philippines, Myanmar, Pakistan, and other Persian Gulf countries. These workers have become essential to the functioning of the Saudi economy. Virtually all domestic, janitorial, and sanitation jobs are done by foreign workers.

The reason Saudis don't take these low-level jobs is because they don't have to. Government **subsidies** from oil revenue have allowed the government to offer free health care (including prescriptions), education, and pensions, along with direct payments, to most Saudi citizens. Saudis tend not to take jobs if they will not lead to careers in science, engineering, medicine, government planning, or at least middle management in a corporate setting. These are the types of jobs with salaries that pay more than government subsidies.

The Saudi government is working to reduce social benefits over time to bring more Saudis into the labor market. Population growth, spurred by campaigns in the 1970s to get couples to have lots of children, and a decline in oil prices have hurt the government's tax income. The trajectory of population growth will outpace oil revenue growth in the future, threatening the sustainability of the subsidy system—hence the plan to redevelop the Saudi economy while reducing social benefits.

The new crown prince, Mohammed bin Salman, has a future vision that includes Saudis in all labor positions. One of the first steps has been the "Saudization" of retail businesses. Saudi Vision 2030, an ambitious public-policy plan initiated and supported by MbS that seeks to make headway in economic diversity and social progress by the year 2030, has as one of its aims the end of reliance on foreign workers. A first step came on September 11, 2018, when a new law went into effect requiring all retail shops to have a minimum number of Saudi employees.

The law led to the closure of thousands of stores. Laws already in place demanded that retail shops be owned by Saudis. However, not only do some Saudis refuse to work in retail stores, they largely refrain from owning them, especially discount retail stores. At the time of the law's passage, several of these stores were operating under illegal ownership by foreign entities. Instead of risking exposure by employing Saudis, the owners chose to close shop. Most street-vendor retail, which is vital to urban working-class neighborhoods, shuttered as a result of the law.

The upcoming generation in Saudi Arabia likely will not see the same lifestyle options as their parents or grandparents. Young people seem to see the writing on the wall and are more ambitious than previous generations. A 2017 article in *Business Insider* reported that young Saudis are "starting to look for work with new urgency."

IN THE NEWS

New Al-Faisaliah City to Create 1 Million New Jobs

One way to forge a new economy is to build a city. China has had successes and failures with cities that have sprung up in the middle of nowhere. Some of them have spent years sitting empty. But Saudi Arabia has tweaked the idea of creating a city from scratch. It is building this one right next to the city of Medina. More than a suburb, Al-Faisaliah will be a modern city that will serve as a model for future development. The project is expected to create 1 million jobs for Saudi citizens.

Tourism in Saudi Arabia.

A desolate alley due to the closure of retail stores.

Poverty

Saudi Arabia does not report data on its poorest citizens, so no firm numbers exist for how many people live below the poverty line. Estimates by other governments and academic experts speculate that the poverty rate is anywhere between 12 and 25 percent. A 2012 article in the *Washington Post* claimed that between 2 million and 4 million of the country's native population live on less than $530 per month, which is considered poverty level in Saudi Arabia. Social programs created in the 1970s for a population of 6 million now must support three times the number of citizens, plus nominal welfare support for foreign workers.

Poverty is a risky subject for Saudi bloggers. In 2017, Saudi authorities jailed three video bloggers for creating a video showing two sides of Saudi life. As of 2018, a mirrored version of the video can be found on YouTube by searching "Mal3ob 3alena : Poverty in Saudi Arabia English Version."

Many families teeter on the brink of homelessness, another subject that is taboo within the kingdom. The government claims that the homeless are mostly foreign workers who can't or won't go

Although it is a taboo subject, some areas of Saudi Arabia have less than others. Just outside of Mecca, dilapidated structures and garbage littering the streets are commonly seen.

home. American studies have countered that claim with evidence that Saudis are living on the streets of the largest cities.

Single women or women caring for a husband who cannot work face particularly harsh difficulties. Men are required to support their families in Saudi Arabia, but little recourse exists for divorced or abandoned spouses. Women find it hard to get jobs that will support their families in a male-dominated culture that relies heavily on male foreign workers.

Saudi Arabia Bets on American Tech for Its Future

The crown prince has a plan for the future that depends on American success. Many of the apps that are commonly used on smartphones owe their existence to Saudi investment. Uber and many others have benefited from Saudi Arabia's commitment to invest in technology as a way to expand its oil-based economy. The success of the United Arab Emirates and its largest city, Dubai, is in part because of investments made in American technology in the 1990s. Saudi Arabia looks to follows a similar growth pattern.

Agriculture

Though it's thought of as a desert, parts of Saudi Arabia are perfect for growing a variety of foods and raising livestock. Wheat, barley, dates, and some citrus grow well in areas of the country around Mecca. Chickens and lamb are dietary staples and a top livestock export. Saudi agriculture accounts for around 5 percent of the economy, up from 3 percent in the 1980s. The country has undertaken large engineering projects to reclaim desert for agriculture, expanding the amount of arable land toward levels seen before oil exploration began to cause desertification. The country that once struggled through seasons hoping for enough dates to feed its own people now supplies dates to world humanitarian efforts.

Food will be the kingdom's Achilles heel in its effort to diversify its economy and move away from oil. The world's need for oil in

Dates are a staple food in Saudi Arabia. They are often sold at the market and are consumed by Muslims when breaking their fast.

the late twentieth century gave Saudi Arabia a sense of security and invulnerability. Saudi Arabia is contending with the massive population boom that ensued, along with the international effort to move the world away from petroleum-powered cars. Even with reclamation projects and the success of some agricultural sectors, the country will have to import most of its food for the foreseeable future.

Imports/Exports

Although Saudi Arabia is the nation's largest oil exporter, the kingdom exports other items as well. Its success at developing its oil industry has made it a top producer of certain petroleum-derived products and chemicals like polymers and hydrocarbons.

The kingdom has a few heavy equipment goods that it exports. Even though Saudi Arabia has to import much of its transportation

Grains like wheat and barley are not grown in Saudi Arabia. Instead, these materials are imported from countries like Canada.

equipment like cars, trucks, helicopters, and planes, the country does make and export tugboats, which accounted for 1 percent of its exports in 2016.

Being a desert country, Saudi Arabia imports much of its food. Barley, corn, and rice are the country's top food imports. Medicines and medical products are also widely imported, though part of the country's future development will depend on expansion of the country's domestic medical infrastructure. Tobacco is the country's top perishable import, and automobiles are its biggest heavy equipment and overall import. Surprisingly, women's Western-style clothing is a big import even with dress codes—these dress codes don't apply within the home.

Saudi Arabia is still a net exporter on its trade balance sheet. Even with the country's lack of natural resources, oil exports more than make up for imports by about $32 billion.

Energy

Saudi Arabia is an energy-rich nation that has achieved self-sufficiency in oil, natural gas, and electricity. At the same time, the country has embarked on a public-awareness program that advocates for programmed thermostats. The effort aims to reduce energy consumption by 5 to 10 percent. Though it may seem like Saudi Arabia doesn't have anything to worry about in terms of energy, it is already consuming all of its natural gas output and 25 percent of its oil output.

The electric grid runs on oil, gas, and steam. The Shoaiba III steam power plant is the largest plant of its kind in the Middle East. The Shoaiba complex near the city of Jeddah also houses an oil power plant and a desalination plant. At a United Nations conference in 2012, Saudi Arabia announced plans to produce a third of its power from solar by 2032. Given the landscape's scarce rainfall and desert sunshine, Saudi Arabia has the potential to maintain

Saudi Arabia is continuing its efforts to reduce energy consumption. New power plants continue to be constructed throughout the Kingdom of Saudi Arabia.

its energy powerhouse status into the twenty-second century. In 2018 the country began the preliminary process to build its first nuclear power plant.

The Saudi government gives its people over $40 billion in energy subsidies for everything from electricity to gasoline. A gallon of gas in Saudi Arabia costs around the equivalent of 50 cents. The oil-based economy and world-record energy subsidies make driving a personal vehicle very affordable.

Saudi Arabia is the world's energy breadbasket. Wind power has already been added to the country's list of energy resources. Aramco, the country's most profitable oil company, teamed up with GE in 2016 to deliver the first wind turbine in an experimental program. Modeled after a new and groundbreaking GE turbine, the unit is a test model with design alterations for adaptation to the Saudi climate. Wind power was added to the energy plan by the crown prince and his Saudi Vision 2030 plan. The Saudis hope that technology will solve the problems facing wind turbines in the desert and the difficulties of storing and transmitting wind-based energy.

Saudi Arabia is filled with vast desert lands. It is the perfect place for solar and wind farms.

Gasoline is quite accessible to Saudi citizens.

Text-Dependent Questions

1. What is desalination, and why is it important for Saudi Arabia to develop this technology?

2. What is the name of the Saudi currency?

3. True or false: Saudi Vision 2030 demands that retail stores employ Pakistani citizens.

Research Project

Research plans for the city of Al-Faisaliah, including estimated size; plans for buildings, recreational facilities, and other structures; and the time lines for development and the ways it is being financed. Write a brief report outlining the city development plan from its original concept through its planned completion.

Quality of Life

"Quality of life" is a term that's used often but has about as much consistent meaning as the term "American dream." Everyone would like to live well. What that means is up for debate. Some people believe that living well means owning a mansion and an expensive car. Others think it means a quiet and uncluttered life where the income level doesn't really matter.

So what is the quality of life Saudis have come to look for? For one, it's generally not about careers unless one is passionate, smart, and able to go to school. Saudi youth generally have a lot of free time on their hands. Subsidies from the government mean that most Saudi citizens don't have to work if they don't want to. The system was more generous in the 1970s; strains on programs have

Words to Understand

Developing nation: A nation that does not have the social or physical infrastructure necessary to provide a modern standard of living to its middle- and working-class population.

Malnutrition: A medical condition that occurs because of lack of food, or lack of nutritious food; causes a large number of additional medical conditions.

Reparations: Payments made to someone to make amends for wrongdoing.

A group of women shop for new handbags.

Saudi Arabia's Quality of Life at a Glance

Life Expectancy at Birth	75.7 years
Maternal Mortality Rate	12 deaths/100,000 live births
Infant Mortality Rate	12.1 deaths/1,000 live births
Physician Density	2.57/1,000 population
Prevalence of HIV/AIDS in Adults	<0.1 percent
Prevalence of Obesity in Adults	35.4 percent
Improved Sanitation Facility Access	100 percent of population
Improved Drinking Water Source	Urban: 97 percent of population; rural: 97 percent of population; total: 97 percent of population
Literacy	94.7 percent of population
Electricity Access	98 percent of population
Telecommunications Access	Fixed line: 13 subscriptions per 100 people; cellular: 141 subscriptions per 100 people
Internet Access	73.8 percent of population
Broadcast Media	State run, state controlled with four networks; major market for pan-Arab satellite broadcasters

not permitted compensation to keep up with inflation, and generally Saudis don't receive as much value from the programs as they once did. This leaves young Saudis struggling to determine what they want out of life. Many of them turn to their religion, with extremists waiting in the wings for frustrated youth looking for answers.

Basic Human Needs

Wealthier nations are expected to take care of their less fortunate citizens. Saudi Arabia is still working on breaking out of **developing nation** status, but it has a high per capita income and lots of credit available due to its large oil reserves. The benefit system in the country is generous. That said, the system is strained due to a continuing population boom. The reality of life in Saudi Arabia works a little bit differently for most people than the lives of the royals paraded through state news stories.

Nutrition and Basic Medical Care

Saudi Arabia is teetering on the edge between "developing nation" and "developed nation" status. Per capita income for a developing nation is considered to be $12,000 or less. The per capita income of Saudi Arabia was $54,500 when last measured in 2017. However, per capita income is just one statistic of many that goes into consideration when determining the development status of a country.

One thing that makes Saudi Arabia a "developing" nation is an imbalance in infrastructure between urban and rural areas. Roads and sanitation services in some parts of the country haven't improved much in the last half a century. Government administration and the legal system suffer from corruption and a lack of consistency. All developing nations face these problems, and Saudi Arabia is seeking to remedy its imbalances.

Compared with other developing nations, Saudi Arabia has a low rate of **malnutrition**, experienced by around 10 percent of the general population. Malnutrition in the United States sits at 3 percent, though the United States has more arable acreage per person than does Saudi Arabia. Saudi Arabia hopes to solve its supply problem by expanding research into desert-reclamation science, which seeks to turn desert areas into viable farmland.

The population boom in Saudi Arabia continues. Although it puts a strain on the system, marketplaces are crowded with shopping families.

There are several differences in infrastructure and roadways in Saudi Arabia. On one hand, Saudi Arabia displays a beautiful skyline with crowded roads. On the other, the buildings are dilapidated, and the roads are made of dirt.

The Ministry of Health is in charge of the country's vast public health- care network. Health-care services include preventive, curative, and rehabilitative treatment. Generous public health care has been provided at no cost since 1927, when the future king of Saudi Arabia started a public health department and medical school in what was then known as the Kingdom of Hejaz. Today the government finds itself strained to provide services to a growing population. Foreign workers and citizens who are private-sector employees must pay a share of the cost. Public employees still receive benefits at no cost.

Coverage has few exclusions and includes no-cost pharmaceuticals. Patients have access to state-of-the-art organ transplants, heart surgeries, and cancer treatments. The experience of accessing these treatments comes with long waiting periods, however, which has made private insurance an attractive option.

Water and Sanitation

Providing water to its citizens is a challenge for Saudi Arabia. Desalination has been the solution to the scarcity of water, due to the country's location on a dry desert peninsula combined with the

५ لتر

غ

NG

ماء زمزم
Zamzam Water

مشروع خادم الحرمين الشريفين
لسقيا زمزم

10 LITERS

ماء زمزم
Zamzam Water

THE CUSTODIAN OF THE TWO HOLY
MOSQUES PROJECT FOR ZAMZAM

Although water is difficult to come by, Saudi Arabia does supply pilgrims with Zamzam water
before they return to their respective countries. Zamzam water comes from the Well of Zamzam.
It is said that this source of water is miraculously created by God.

population boom over the last half-century. The only other source of water comes from desert groundwater deposits that will take thousands of years to renew once they are depleted. Only in the mountainous southwest region of the country are there enough lakes to make surface water a supply option. The breakdown of supply sources are 50 percent desalination, 40 percent nonrenewable groundwater, and 10 percent surface water.

Shelter

The traditional nature of Saudi families, with many generations living under the same roof, means that Saudis look for as much space as they can get. The affluent often buy or build compounds that contain two or three villas on the property so several generations of extended family can live together. Even less affluent Saudis will house several generations within a small house or apartment.

A study from 2007 estimated that there were 83,000 homeless children on the streets of Riyadh. The study found that the majority of the children came to Saudi Arabia illegally to work as jockeys

A common residential area in Saudi Arabia.

in camel racing, and when the children got too old, they were sent to work in retail stores. There they were typically treated poorly, and many ran away for a life on the streets.

The Saudi government has built shelters for workers, many of whom have had their passports confiscated by employers. Without a passport the workers cannot return to their home country. Employers often take passports as a way to retain workers. Because the stranded foreign workers are putting a strain on an already strained social safety net, the employers are now facing investigations from Saudi authorities who turned a blind eye to the practice for many years.

Personal Safety

Youth unemployment and poor conditions for foreign workers have been blamed for a growing trend of petty crimes, theft, and robbery. Once upon a time in the 1970s, the kingdom could claim to be just about 100 percent crime free. Through the 1990s the crime rate increased over 400 percent. Between the years of 2012 and 2013, the petty crime rate more than doubled. The U.S. State Department warns travelers that terrorist-related kidnappings remain a threat.

Reports of major crimes like murder and rape are in the fractions of a percent, typically around .010 per 100,000 people. However, those statistics are disputed by the United Nations. The UN reported a murder rate of 1.5 per 100,000 population in 2015; most of these crimes were determined to be drug related. Rape is considered vastly underreported in the kingdom. Often the woman involved is blamed and given prison time and lashings along with, or instead of, the accused.

Traffic accidents in Saudi Arabia are a problem, with 8,000 traffic-related deaths a year. By contrast, the United States suffers around 30,000 deaths per year from traffic accidents. When accounting for population differences, the death rate in Saudi Arabia is twice that of the United States. Auto accidents are also a burden on the criminal justice system. Everyone involved in an accident is immediately imprisoned until the responsible party can be determined, and **reparations** paid to the victims.

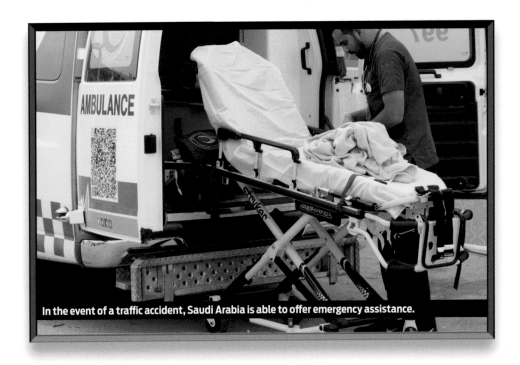
In the event of a traffic accident, Saudi Arabia is able to offer emergency assistance.

Personal Well-Being

Many products and services that we have taken for granted in the Western world for generations were first introduced to Saudi society as recently as the 1960s and 1970s. This includes availability of doctors and medicine, education, housing, and even shopping. A Saudi citizen in the 1960s was likely born to a nomadic tribe. The changes the average Saudi of that generation saw in his or her lifetime are similar to the changes seen by the American generation of the late nineteenth century, going from a rural lifestyle caring for livestock to an urban one caring for a nice automobile. Although Saudi Arabia made great strides in providing services to its citizens and rapidly expanding cities and commerce, imbalances in access vary from region to region and among social classes.

Education

Saudi schools are open to every citizen for instruction from the preschool through college level. Generous government subsidies are provided to every school, both public and private. Public schools are fully funded by the government. Private schools have

Schoolchildren take part in a science lesson.

their administration costs covered in addition to having access to government grants.

The Saudi government began its university system back in the 1950s, seeing a need for educated workers in the burgeoning oil economy. Although Saudi universities are subsidized and just about any citizen who wants to go to college gets a slot, the country still imports workers to do high-skilled tech, engineering, and management jobs. In this environment, Saudis occupy the upper-management positions, and foreign workers fill the middle- and lower-management positions in Saudi companies. Universities have been criticized for requiring excessive religious instruction and relying on rote memorization for subjects that require critical thinking skills.

Information Access

Saudi Arabia has a world-class internet infrastructure in its cities, whereas rural areas lag behind, using slow dial-up or expensive satellite connections. A government initiative aims to have broadband available in most rural areas by 2022. Internet access rose to almost

A group of college students prepare for an exam.

Cellular phones and the internet are easily accessible in Saudi Arabia, yet the information that is released to the public is heavily censored.

30 million users in 2018. More than 90 percent of Saudi Arabia is now hooked up to the internet. But although most of the country has internet access, the Saudi internet is one of the most censored in the world.

The vast moral and political censorship of the internet contrasts with the supreme effort the country has put into getting people online. The new crown prince has made it his personal cause to make affordable internet available to everyone, but the religious police and intelligence services are keeping lists of sites censored on moral, religious, or political grounds. The result has been the expected blocks not only on adult sites and ISIS-supporter sites but on Western fashion and Christian sites as well. All Israeli sites and almost all sites related to Judaism and Jewish causes are blocked.

A backlash on social media has become active because of the censorship, with Egypt being the only Middle Eastern country with more bloggers than Saudi Arabia. Many of the Saudi bloggers are women who use pseudonyms and proxy servers to prevent

Computer lessons are given in school, but access to certain information is limited.

their identities from being uncovered. Many have received prison sentences of 10 years or more by advocating for social change. Even advocating for wearing Western fashion can get a person into trouble.

Health and Wellness

Saudi Arabia has a national health-care system that provides primary care and specialty services to Saudi citizens. All non-Saudi citizens working in the country are required to purchase health insurance.

Life expectancy in 1963 was a short 45 years. In the more than five decades since then, improvements in health care and the establishment of social services has lifted life expectancy to 75 years. This is four and a half years greater than the UN's global average of 70.5 years.

Environment

Years of dedication to pumping and refining as much oil as possible has led to environmental apathy in Saudi Arabia. The country's environmental plan seemed to be to have no plan at all. This policy led to desertification of precious arable land (though much of it is being reclaimed), pollution problems in urban areas, and increased environmental hydrocarbons caused by an oil spill during the first Gulf War. Testing done in 2017 showed that in the 25 years since the Gulf War spill, biodiversity of seabed habitats has been permanently changed by the presence of oil residue.

Though Saudi Arabia has had a history of ignoring environmental issues, a renewed "green" effort has been initiated as part of the Saudi Vision 2030 program. Both renewable energy and environmental sustainability programs are folded into the massive plan.

Opportunity

Opportunity in Saudi Arabia depends on how one defines the term. Foreign workers fleeing poverty, war, and social problems find the opportunity to make enough money to support family back home. Saudis have a wide range of educational opportunities, but the religious nature of the schools takes away from learning practical skills. Employers prefer foreign workers for technical positions

even when Saudis are available and willing to do the work because of a lack of analytical and critical thinking skills.

Personal and Political Rights

Saudi Arabia bases its system of laws on its interpretation of Sharia law. A clear set of rules is established for every category of life, and no deviation is tolerated. In fact, the state has an obligation to correct those who deviate. This has led to categories of crime that are strange to those used to the concepts of freedom of thought and action. The categories have names like personal belief crimes, violations against intellect, and worship violations.

A cause for arrest in Saudi Arabia.

No guarantee of personal or political rights exists in Saudi Arabia. Bloggers are jailed for actions that wouldn't even garner a sideways glance from a classmate in most of the world. Singers and athletes have gotten in trouble with the law for making a gesture believed to be associated with drug use, an offense that wouldn't even be relegated to late-night television in the United States. The banned gesture is a hip-hop dance move called dabbing, where a dancer tucks his or her face inside the crook of their arm. Saudi authorities believe the dance move references marijuana culture.

Saudi citizens can be easily tracked. National ID cards are necessary to do almost any kind of business in Saudi Arabia, such as entering a school, checking into a hotel room, renting an apartment, and entering the country. When the ID cards are swiped, the holder's position information becomes available to the police.

The Tragedy of Jamal Khashoggi

The dominant news story around Saudi Arabia at the end of 2018 was undoubtedly the killing of dissident journalist Jamal Khashoggi at the Saudi consulate in Istanbul, Turkey, in October. Khashoggi had been living in the United States at the time of his death, where he authored a weekly column for the *Washington Post*. His outspoken criticism of the Saudi royal family and Mohammed bin Salman likely drew the ire of Saudi leaders.

For weeks, the details around the story were unclear. All that was known was that on October 2nd, Khashoggi walked into the consulate to obtain some legal documents and never emerged. Turkish officials said that a team of Saudi agents, some of whom had ties to Mohammed bin Salman, entered Turkey in the days before the murder. Turkish officials said that one of these agents had brought a bone saw into the country.

The Saudis denied any wrongdoing, first saying that Khashoggi had, in fact, left the consulate, then switching their story to blame "rogue officials" for carrying out the murder. Further inconsistencies in the account cast doubt on the crown prince and his associates.

The international community began to demand answers. In November, the Turkish government released audio recordings of the killing to officials in Saudi Arabia, the United States, the United Kingdom, and France. The U.S. Central Intelligence Agency concluded that bin Salman was behind Khashoggi's death shortly after hearing the recordings.

Citing the U.S. business relationships with Saudi Arabia, particularly in the realm of arms sales, U.S. President Donald Trump stunned the international community when he stood by bin Salman's claims of innocence in the autumn and winter of 2018. In December, the U.S. Senate voted to end U.S. participation in the war in Yemen and passed a unanimous measure to name bin Salman as responsible for Khashoggi's death. The actions were seen as a clear rebuke of Trump's embrace of the Saudi dictatorship.

Until recently women were not allowed to drive in Saudi Arabia. The only country in the world to have a ban on female drivers lifted its prohibition on July 24, 2018. However, though the government liberalized its driving laws, the police decided they needed to send the message that although the government may have been wrong, they were still right. They proceeded to round up activists in the country who had been working toward lifting the ban. Several prominent activists were arrested and charged with undermining state security. On the other side of the political spectrum, the government felt it was necessary to pass a law saying that no one was allowed to harass a woman because she was driving. Several radical religious figures had advocated harming female drivers in the days leading up to the change.

Freedom of Choice

Abortion is illegal throughout the kingdom with exceptions to save the life of the mother or if the pregnancy threatens the mental health of the mother. Specific rules state that a couple's financial insecurity is not a valid reason to request an abortion. Though some Islamic schools of thought believe abortion is permissible, the view within Wahhabism is that abortion is *haram*, which means forbidden, under Islamic law.

Tolerance and Inclusion

Homosexuality and transgenderism are illegal in Saudi Arabia. Punishment varies depending on the circumstances. The typical sentence is several years of confinement followed by several hundred lashes. Those convicted of transgender activities combined with homosexuality receive the harshest sentences. In 2009, police raided a party and arrested 67 men who were found to be cross-dressing, and in 2016 an internet celebrity was arrested in the city of Qassim for cross-dressing online. One man who was found to be meeting other men via Twitter was given a sentence of three years in prison and 450 lashes. Human rights organizations such as Human Rights Watch have decried the harsh treatment of the LGBTQ population in Saudi Arabia.

Higher Education

The first modern university in the Persian Gulf was opened in Riyadh in 1957. The King Saud University accepts male and female students seeking to study natural sciences, humanities, professional studies, and medicine. Women are taught separately from men and must meet with male advisors through videoconferencing.

The country has 24 government universities that offer bachelor's, master's, and doctoral degrees in the sciences and humanities. A Wahhabi-based curriculum dominates the public schools. Students must memorize large parts of the Qu'ran and study how to integrate Islamic tradition into everyday life. Human Rights Watch has issued a report showing that religious curricula in Saudi schools fosters hate against the country's Shi'a minority as well as Jews and other non-Muslims.

King Saud University.

Higher Education for Women

The main purpose of opening up higher education to women in Saudi Arabia was to make them competitive with foreign women as wives. Sometimes change comes begrudgingly, and that's the circumstance under which women got to go to college in Saudi Arabia. In the 1970s, as Saudi Arabia was beginning to dominate the world's oil production, the country sent many of its young men to study in Europe and America. More than a few of them came back with wives. This led to a crisis within the Saudi religious and governmental hierarchy. Saudi women, it seemed, were not educated enough to attract Saudi husbands. The solution was to let Saudi women go to college.

Text-Dependent Questions

1. Describe what happens to people involved in a traffic accident in Saudi Arabia.

2. True or false: Writing about wanting to wear Western fashion can get a blogger arrested in Saudi Arabia.

3. Explain the effect religious studies are having on employers' views of Saudi workers.

Research Project

Research the types of articles that have gotten journalists in trouble in Saudi Arabia. Then try your own hand at it: Select a policy or area of public life where you disagree with the Saudi government's approach, and write a short article stating your opinion, backed with reasons and evidence. Share your work with a parent or teacher.

CHAPTER 5

Society and Culture

Saudi Arabia modernized in a comparative blink of an eye. Between 1930—around the time oil was discovered on the peninsula—and 1980, the country expanded cities, established infrastructure like electricity and sanitation, built a media network, taught most of its people to read, and became one of the world's dominant nations.

Like a character in a time-travel story, the Saudi nation seems left with a case of vertigo. Some aspects of tribal culture remain, especially with social attitudes toward women. The country remains entrenched in an excessively bureaucratic and complex government system. People are socially defined by their race and immigration status. Punishments for minor crimes can be harsh.

Young people of Saudi Arabia appear to be ready to create major change in their culture. Right now Saudi Arabian society is transforming. Demands have led to recent changes in the status of women and the powers of the religious police. At the same time, traditionalists remain within the power structure. The current easing

Words to Understand

Authoritarianism: Used to describe a type of government or rule that enforces strict adherence to leaders and laws.

Dialect: Variation in a language demonstrated by differences in vocabulary and grammar, unlike an accent, which is a variation in tone only.

Mutaween: The common name of the religious police in Saudi Arabia.

Children in the mosque reading the Qu'ran.

Saudi Arabia's Society and Culture at a Glance

Population	28,571,770 (July 2017 est.)
Population Rank	47
Sex Ratio	1.19 males/females
Age Distribution	26.1 percent age 0–14; 18.57 percent age 15–24; 46.86 percent age 25–54; 5.03 percent age 55–64; 3.44 percent age 65 and over
Ethnic Groups	Arab 90 percent, Afro-Asian 10 percent
Religions	Muslim (official); other religions are prohibited
Languages	Arabic

of cultural restrictions that make Saudi Arabia an outlier among nations could continue, or the country's traditionalist leadership could force the country to abolish those changes, returning it to an even stricter **authoritarianism**.

Birth and Death Rates

The birth rate in Saudi Arabia is 15.6 births per 1,000 people, and the death rate is 3.3 deaths per 1,000 people. Infant mortality stands at 12.1 deaths per 1,000 live births, less than half the global average of 30.5. The country ranks 108th in infant mortality worldwide. The fertility rate of Saudi females saw a considerable decline between 2004 and 2014. Saudi women averaged 3.6 childbirths in a lifetime in 2004. That figure declined to 2.04 by 2018.

That figure isn't low enough for some Saudi experts, however. Concerns over city crowding, the environmental impacts of climate change and coastal development, and the rising cost of living have led to calls for measures to further reduce population growth. Others say the lower birth rate is the problem and want Saudi women to

Saudi Arabia ranks 108th in infant mortality worldwide.

have more children so the country can be less reliant on foreign workers.

The reasons for the lower birth rate seem to be a combination of things. Saudi women find it easier to get an education than they did several decades ago, allowing more women to focus on their careers while they delay starting families. The rising cost of living has increased demand for abortions, though they remain illegal except for health reasons. Couples are tending to delay expanding their families, with siblings being added every two years instead of every year, as occurred a decade ago.

Population by Age

Saudi Arabia is a country of young people. Over half its people are under the age of 25. The average age of the Saudi population is 29.8 years. By contrast, the average age of the U.S. population is 37.8 years. The young population of Saudi Arabia is due to the culture's unique escalation from a nomadic people to petroleum professionals in two generations. Once Saudis were seen as a violent nuisance to

The average age of Saudis is 29.8 years old. Many of these young Saudis enjoy group activities like attending Saudi football games featuring the national team.

British soldiers partitioning what was left of the Ottoman Empire after World War I. Five decades later Saudi Arabia brought America to a halt with an oil embargo, its power secured by the support of other oil-producing nations through an organization called OPEC, which was created by the Saudis themselves.

The speed at which Saudi Arabia transformed into a powerhouse explains why it has so many young people today. Back in the early 1960s, when the country was midway through developing its oil industry, the average life expectancy was about 46 years. Today, the figure sits at a world-class 75 years. However, the climb in life expectancy happened over several decades, with fewer people dying at younger ages every year. During these decades, newfound prosperity allowed Saudis to have bigger families. People dying at younger ages throughout the mid-twentieth century combined with a "baby boom" set up today's youth-oriented demographics.

Like many nations in the Persian Gulf, Saudi Arabia has a gender imbalance. The ratio of men to women is 1.19 males to one female. That's not as much as in the neighboring country of the United Arab Emirates, where for every one woman there are 2.18 men, or the world record holder, Qatar, which has a male to female ratio of 3.41 to one.

Religions

Saudi Arabia is a theocratic state as well as an absolute monarchy. Contrary to popular belief, no law exists that requires anyone to be a follower of any particular form of Islam. But by virtue of the political power of the religious scholars and the street power of their religious police, it is difficult if not impossible to be a Saudi citizen who is not a follower of Wahhabi Islam.

The **mutaween**, as the religious police are known, make sure that Wahhabi practices are observed in public, and that no religion other than Islam may have a public presence in any form, from a Buddhist temple with street signage to a handful of Christians praying in a restaurant. Technically, private practice of another religion is permitted; however, the *mutaween* have a reputation for breaking up Christian gatherings in the homes of foreign workers.

Although Saudi Arabia may tolerate other religious practices in private, it permits only adherents of Wahhabism to hold any kind

A group of Wahhabis sit in a mosque and listen to the teachings of an imam.

of official office or government rank. The country has been accused of practicing religious apartheid. Though less than 40 percent of those who live in Saudi Arabia follow Wahhabism, they benefit from social and economic practices that grant them access to better education, jobs, and homes.

Non-Muslim travelers have been able to freely bring in personal religious materials since 2013. Yet this does not apply to the Shi'a minority in northeast Saudi Arabia. Religious materials originating from Iran are often confiscated, because Iranian influence is considered a threat to stability by the Saudi government.

Ethnic Groups

The vast majority of Saudi citizens are Arabs, around 90 percent. The rest are of Afro-Asian descent. The Afro-Asian population are ex-slaves and descendants of ex-slaves. Saudi Arabia abolished slavery in 1962 at the urging of the United States and Britain. Although slaves received their freedom, they did not receive full citizenship, and laws in place today prohibit members of the group from holding government positions.

About a third of those who reside in Saudi Arabia are guest workers from other nations. They come to Saudi Arabia from Asian countries such as Pakistan, Nepal, Myanmar, the Philippines, and Sri Lanka. South Koreans were the most common foreign workers in the 1970s. Today, South Korea is a prosperous nation that itself has a growing reliance on foreign workers.

The neighboring countries of the United Arab Emirates and Kuwait both take advantage of cheap labor from North Korea, but Saudi Arabia has avoided using North Koreans. Use of North Korean workers by foreign nations has brought criticism from the United States. The workers are not paid directly. They are given an expense allowance, but all other money is sent to the North Korean government.

Languages

Arabic is the official language of Saudi Arabia. Like most languages Arabic has numerous **dialects**, three of which are spoken in Saudi Arabia. Official government communications and the national media use Modern Standard Arabic. Regionally, Saudis speak Najdi, Hejazi, and Gulf Arabic.

Najdi is spoken in the central part of the country and contains several subdialects. One of them, Central Najdi, is spoken in the capital of Riyadh. The dialect is spoken in farming communities around the city, and use of the subdialect is seen as a sign of urban sophistication.

The remaining nomadic people of Saudi Arabia have their own dialect called Badawi Najdi. This is the oldest dialect in Saudi Arabia, dating back to the thirteenth century. It is so similar to the nomadic dialects of the wider Arab world that Saudi television shows in Badawi Najdi are preferred to other Arab television shows in native nomadic languages. Even though the Saudi shows are in a different dialect, they are preferred over the native shows because of higher-value writing, acting, special effects, and production.

Hejazi is the country's western dialect. It is spoken in and around Mecca. About half of Saudi citizens speak in the Hejazi dialect. Two subdialects consist of urban and rural variations.

Gulf Arabic is spoken around the Persian Gulf area of the country. It is the dialect spoken by many members of the Shi'a minority. Like

the urban sophistication of Central Najdi, Gulf Arabic announces the geographical origin of its speaker by its tone. Unlike Central Najdi, however, the tone indicates one is a member of a shunned minority instead of announcing urban credentials.

Berber is the language of Saudi Arabia's former slave population. The Afro-Asian minority, who were granted their freedom in 1963 but not full Saudi citizenship, live mostly in ghettoized areas of major cities. Berber is becoming an important language in Saudi Arabian hip-hop. The musical form that evolved out of American urban decay is now influencing Saudi Arabia's own marginalized community. Just like it did in America, hip-hop is impacting the wider Saudi youth culture and shining a light on social problems.

IN THE NEWS

Hip-Hop Resonates with Marginalized Saudi Youth

Jason Nichols is an American academic in African American studies who focuses on hip-hop culture. He got to travel to Saudi Arabia with American rap artists on a state department cultural exchange. He reported on the connection he made with Afro-Asian youth, who make up 10 percent of the Saudi population. They have found inspiration in American hip-hop artists who share similar tales of being marginalized. "*Tarsh*" is the racial slur most commonly thrown at the Saudi Afro-Asian community. Saudis joke that the "*tarsh*" came for Hajj and didn't have the money to return home. The truth is that most of these young people are the grandchildren or great-grandchildren of slaves who received their freedom only in 1963. The American hip-hop artist most popular with the young people Nichols met was by far Tupac.

About a third of the people residing in the country speak none of the above languages. They are guest workers from all over the world. Some of the more common languages heard on factory floors or in the kitchens of wealthy households are Tagalog, Rohingya, and Urdu. Tagalog is the language of the Philippines, and Filipinos make up the majority of foreign workers. Rohingya is spoken by people from the same population currently being displaced from Myanmar. Urdu is spoken by Pakistani foreign workers who make up a large portion of Saudi Arabia's corporate managers.

Foods

The basic cuisine of Saudi Arabia hasn't changed in a thousand years. Dietary staples include lamb, chicken, rice, wheat, yogurt, coffee, and dates. Mutabbaq is a favorite lunch and afternoon snack. A relative of the sandwich, mutabbaq is fried bread stuffed with any assortment of meat and veggies. It's become popular throughout the Middle East and into India.

A street vendor prepares mutabbaq.

Kabsa.

Kabsa is a chicken-and-rice dish seasoned with saffron, the most expensive spice in the world. The dish is seasoned with a combination of saffron, cinnamon, black lime, cardamom, nutmeg, and bay leaves.

Shawarma is the Saudi version of barbeque. It's marinated meat, usually sheep or chicken, cooked on a skewer over an open fire. The difference between shawarma and kabobs are that kabobs are pieces of chicken cooked on a skewer over an open fire, and shawarma is the process of skewering and cooking the whole chicken.

Mofatah is a delicacy in Saudi Arabia. This cumin and cardamom–based lamb dish is a difficult one to master and is reserved for special occasions. The lamb should be very fresh and tender. Many restaurants will prepare mofatah only if patrons bring their own lamb.

Shawarma being cooked and skewered.

Falafel is the Saudi dish that everyone's heard of. It's a fried ball of chickpeas and fava beans that can be spiced in various ways. It's quick to make, so it's a favorite Saudi dinner on those nights when everyone is going out.

National Holidays

Saudi Arabia recognizes only three national holidays and numerous optional holidays in which only public-sector employees are guaranteed days off. The three national holidays are Eid al-Fitr (the end of Ramadan), Eid al-Adha (Feast of Sacrifice), and National Day, which is the day of the founding of the kingdom, September 23rd. Eid

Falafel can be served in a number of ways. Many people will eat it as a sandwich with the falafel balls served in a pita.

Saudi men dressed in traditional clothing perform a folk dance in celebration of Eid al-Fitr.

Men trim buffalo cow meat to be distributed during Eid al-Adha.

The Saudi military celebrates National Day.

Movie Theaters Reopen in Saudi Arabia

Movie theaters were banned in Saudi Arabia since shortly after the Grand Mosque seizure in 1982. Religious authorities were trying to purge the country of all non-Wahhabi influences, and many things across the cultural spectrum were outlawed. Although movie theaters were absent from Saudi social life, video stories and satellite pay-per-view movies remained available. In April 2018 the country formally lifted the ban with an exclusive screening of Marvel's *Black Panther* at a new movie theater in Riyadh.

Learn more about the Hajj.

al-Fitr celebrates the end of fasting for Ramadan, which is observed during the month that the Qu'ran was revealed to Muhammad. Eid al-Adha celebrates obedience to God with a remembrance of the story of Abraham sacrificing his son. As with many holidays on the Islamic calendar, which is based on the lunar calendar, they can fall one day before or after the dates stated on Western calendars.

Text-Dependent Questions

1. Explain why Saudi Arabia has so many young people.

2. What language has become important in Saudi Arabian hip-hop?

3. Name the three national holidays in Saudi Arabia.

Research Project

How has hip-hop culture affected Saudi Arabia? Research how the musical style is influencing the wider, more traditional culture. Write an article on what hip-hop means to Saudi youth. Some things to think about: Are authorities tolerating performances and recordings? Is hip-hop mixing with traditional music of the area? Who are the country's top artists, and how many of them are female?

Series Glossary of Key Terms

Absolute monarchy: A form of government led by a single individual, usually called a king or a queen, who has control over all aspects of government and whose authority cannot be challenged.

Amendment: A change to a nation's constitution or political process, sometimes major and sometimes minor.

Arable: Describing land that is capable of being used for agriculture.

Asylum: When a nation grants protection to a refugee or immigrant who has been persecuted in his or her own country.

Austerity: Governmental policies that include spending cuts, tax increases, or a combination of the two, with the aim of reducing budget deficits.

Authoritarianism: Governmental structure in which all citizens must follow the commands of the reigning authority, with few or no rights of their own.

Autocracy: Ruling regime in which the leader has absolute power.

Bicameral: A legislative body structured into two branches or chambers.

Bilateral: Something that involves two nations or parties.

Bloc: A group of countries or parties with similar aims and purposes.

Cash crop: Agriculture meant to be sold directly for profit rather than consumed.

Central bank: A government-authorized bank whose purpose is to provide money to retail, commercial, investment, and other banks.

Cleric: A general term for a religious leader such as a priest or imam.

Coalition force: A force made up of military elements from nations that have created a temporary alliance for a specific purpose.

Colonization: The process of occupying land and controlling a native population.

Commodities: Raw products of agriculture or mining, such as corn or precious metals, that can be bought and sold on the market.

Communism: An economic and political system where all property is held in common; a form of government in which a one-party state controls the means of production and distribution of resources.

Conscription: Compulsory enlistment into state service, usually the military.

Constituency: A body of voters in a specific area who elect a representative to a legislative body.

Constitution: A written document or unwritten set of traditions that outline the powers, responsibilities, and limitations of a government.

Coup: A quick change in government leadership without a legal basis, most often by violent means.

De-escalation: Reduction or elimination of armed hostilities in a war zone, often directed by a cease-fire or truce.

Defector: A citizen who flees his or her country, often out of fear of oppression or punishment, to start a life in another country.

Demilitarized zone: An area where military personnel, installations, and related activities are prohibited.

Depose: The act of removing a head of government through force, intimidation, and/or manipulation.

Détente: An easing of hostility or strained relations, particularly between countries.

Developing nation: A nation that does not have the social or physical infrastructure necessary to provide a modern standard of living to its middle- and working-class population.

Diaspora: The members of a community that spread out into the wider world, sometimes assimilating to new cultures and sometimes retaining most or all of their original culture.

Diktat: An order from an authority given without popular approval.

Disenfranchise: To take away someone's rights.

Displaced persons: Persons who are forced to leave their home country or a region of their country due to war, persecution, or natural disasters.

Economic boom: A period of rapid economic and financial growth, resulting in greater wealth and more purchasing power.

Economic reserves: Currency, usually in the form of gold, used to support the paper money distributed through an economy, available to be used by a government when its own currency does not have enough value.

Edict: A proclamation by a person in authority that functions the same as a law.

Embargo: An official ban on trade.

Federation: A country formed by separate states with a central government that manages national and international affairs, but control over local matters is retained by individual states.

Food insecurity: Being without reliable access to nutritious food at an affordable price and in sufficient quantity.

Free-floating currency: A currency whose value is determined by the free market, changing according to supply and demand for that currency.

Fundamentalist: A political and/or religious ideology based explicitly on traditional orthodox concepts, with rejection of modern values.

Gross Domestic Product (GDP): The total value of goods and services a country produces in a given time frame.

Hegemony: Dominance of one nation over others.

Heretical: When someone's beliefs contradict an orthodox religion.

Indigenous: Referring to a person or group native to a particular place.

Industrialization: The transition from an agricultural economy to a manufacturing economy.

Inflation: A general increase in prices and a decrease in the purchasing value of money.

Insurgency: An organized movement aimed at overthrowing or destroying a government.

Islamist: A military or political organization that believes in the fundamentals of Islam as the guiding principle, rather than secular law; often used synonymously (although not always accurately) with Islamic terrorism.

Jihad: A struggle or exertion on behalf of Islam, sometimes through armed conflict.

Judiciary: A network of courts within a society and their relationship to each other.

Mercantilism: A historical economic theory that focuses on the trade of raw materials from a colony to the mother country, and of manufactured goods from the mother country to the colony, for the profit of the mother country.

Migrant: A person who moves from place to place, either by choice or due to warfare or other economic, political, or environmental crises.

Militia: A group of volunteer soldiers who do not fight with a military full-time.

Municipal elections: Elections held for office on the local level, such as town, city, or county.

Nationalize: When an industry or sector of the economy is totally owned and operated by the government.

Parliamentary: Governmental structure in which executive power is awarded to a cabinet of legislative body members, rather than elected by the people directly.

Paramilitary: Semimilitarized force, trained in tactics and organized by rank, but not officially part of a nation's formal military.

Patriarchy: A system of society or government in which power is held by men.

Police state: Nation in which the state closely monitors activity and harshly punishes any citizen thought to be critical of society or the government.

Populism: An approach to politics, often with authoritarian elements, that emphasizes the role of ordinary people in a society's government over that of an elite class.

Propagandist: A person who disseminates government-created communications, like TV shows and posters, that seek to directly influence and control a national audience to serve the needs of the government, sometimes employing outright falsehoods.

Proportional representation: An electoral system in which political parties gain seats in proportion to the number of votes cast for those seats.

Protectionist: Actions on behalf of a government to stem international trade in favor of helping domestic businesses and producers.

Reactionary: A person who opposes new social and economic ideas or reforms; a person who seeks a return to past forms of governance.

Referendum: A decision on a particular issue put up to a popular vote.

Refugee: A person who leaves his or her home nation, by force or by choice, to flee from war or oppression.

Reparations: Payments made to someone to make amends for wrongdoing.

Republicanism: A political philosophy of representative government in which citizens elect leaders to govern.

Rubber-stamp legislature: Legislative body with formal authority but little, if any, decision-making power and subordinate to another branch of government or political party leadership.

Sanctions: Political and/or economic punishments levied against another nation as punishment for wrongdoing.

Secretariat: A permanent administrative office or department, usually in government, and the staff of that office or department.

Sect: A subgroup of a major religion, with individual beliefs or philosophies that divide it from other subgroups of the religion.

Sovereignty: The ability of a country to rule itself.

Statute: A law created and passed by a legislative body.

Subsidies: Amounts of money that a government gives to a particular industry to help manage prices or promote social or economic policies.

Tariff: A tax or fee placed on imported or exported products.

Theocratic: Of or relating to a theocracy, a form of government that lays claim to God as the source and justification of its authority.

Totalitarian: A form of government where power is in the hands of a single person or group.

Trade deficit: The degree to which a country must buy more imports than it sells exports; can reflect economic problems as well as strong buying power.

Trade surplus: The degree to which a country can sell more exports than it purchases; can reflect economic strength as well as poor buying power.

Welfare state: A system where the government publically funds programs to ensure the health and well-being of its citizens.

Chronology of Key Events

570	The Prophet Muhammad is born in the city of Mecca.
629	Muhammad controls both Mecca and Medina; Islamic caliphate era begins.
900	Sharifate of Mecca establishes a state comprising Mecca, Medina, and the surrounding areas between the two cities so to ensure stable political control for Islam's holiest cities and the annual Hajj pilgrimage.
1517	Ottoman Empire begins its conquest of the Arabian Peninsula.
1744	The first member of the al-Saud family to lead a territory, Muhammad Ibn Saud, rises to power in the area around Riyadh; he becomes a leading figure in the Wahhabi movement.
1816	The al-Saud family conquers most of what is today Saudi Arabia.
1818	The Ottoman Sultan, through the viceroy of Egypt, removes Ibn Saud from power in a quick series of battles.
1824	The al-Saud family returns to power in a smaller region within the interior of the peninsula.
1891	The al-Saud family is sent into exile in Kuwait by the rival al-Rashid family.
1902	The al-Saud family returns from exile to lead a patchwork area of tribal lands.
1924	British support the al-Saud family to consolidate and lead a larger kingdom in the area, which becomes the Kingdom of Najd.
1927	King Muhammad Ibn Saud merges Najd with the Kingdom of Hejaz, forming the Kingdom of Hejaz and Najd.
1932	Establishment of the Kingdom of Saudi Arabia with the merger of the two kingdoms under Muhammad Ibn Saud as Saudi Arabia's first king.
1938	After almost a decade of successful oil discovery in emirates surrounding Saudi Arabia, oil is discovered along the Persian Gulf coast of the country after much hardship, including several oil well cave-ins.
1940	Saudi oil industry begins decades of rapid growth, with demand at an all-time high due to World War II.

1952	Arab cold war begins when the king of Egypt is overthrown by an Egyptian military officer named Gamal Abdel Nasser; Nasser begins a campaign of pan-Arab socialism that Saudi Arabia aggressively opposes.
1953	King Saud succeeds his father and becomes the second king of Saudi Arabia.
1962	The first Yemeni conflict begins when President Nasser of Egypt sends troops into Yemen to support anti-monarchy rebels; Saudi Arabia does not enter Yemen but gives support to the Yemeni monarch.
1973	Saudi Arabia leads Arab oil embargo, mainly focused on the United States due to its support of Israel, which causes transportation disruptions across the world.
1981	The Grand Mosque is seized for two weeks by a religious group claiming its leader is the Twelfth Imam whose coming is foretold in the Qu'ran.
1990	Saudi Arabia allows foreign troops on its soil for the first time in preparation for the Gulf War, which Saudi Arabia fully participates in.
2005	King Abdullah succeeds his brother King Fahd and begins a period of reform.
2015	King Salman succeeds his brother King Abdullah and accelerates the kingdom's reform, drawing scorn from religious leaders.
2015	Current Yemeni conflict begins as two governments claim to be the legitimate government of Yemen; one side is supported by Saudi Arabia and the other by Iran.
2017	King Salman declares Muhammed bin Salman, his son, the crown prince and heir apparent, delegating much of his authority to him; bin Salman uses authority to begin a brutal crackdown on government officials under the banner of an anti-corruption campaign.

Further Reading & Internet Resources

Books

House Elliot, Karen. *On Saudi Arabia: Its People, Past, Religion, Fault Lines—and Future*. Reprint Edition. New York: Vintage, 2013. The former publisher of the *Wall Street Journal* recounts her personal history as a foreign correspondent in the kingdom and also shares her perspective on the history and future of Saudi Arabia.

Lacey, Robert. *Inside the Kingdom: Kings, Clerics, Modernists, Terrorists, and the Struggle for Saudi Arabia*. New York City: Penguin, 2009. The author of this book is a British historian who has worked in Saudi Arabia off and on since the 1979 Grand Mosque seizure. His account chronicles the dynamics of the Saudi culture at all levels of society.

Moss, Walkaboutdude D. *A Saudi Hospital in the Empty Quarters: An American Respiratory Therapist Account Living in the Kingdom of Saudi Arabia*. Laughing Mystic Books, 2009. An American medical practitioner recounts his experience living and working in Saudi Arabia.

Reidel, Bruce. *Kings and Presidents: Saudi Arabia and the United States since FDR*. Washington, DC: Brookings Institution Press, 2017. In this look at U.S.-Saudi relations since World War II, the author covers the rocky relationship between the world's largest democracy and one of the last absolute monarchies from the administrations of FDR to Donald Trump.

Stair, Nancy. *A Historical Atlas of Saudi Arabia*. New York: Rosen Publishing Group, 2003. This book of maps follows the history of Saudi Arabia as the country moves from backward Ottoman province to the world's top oil producer.

Web Sites

Saudi National Portal. *https://www.saudi.gov.sa. This website has full information on government services, organizations, rules and laws, and labor and social development issues of Saudi Arabia.*

Arab News. *http://www.arabnews.com. Arab News is a Saudi-based newspaper and the largest English-language news daily in the country. Its website covers stories across all of the Middle East.*

Freedom House. *https://freedomhouse.org. Freedom House is an international organization promoting democracy and freedom. Its website has a database assessing human rights in various countries.*

Human Rights Watch. *https://www.hrw.org. Human Rights Watch is one of the world's leading organizations tracking rights abuses around the world. Its website contains content about human rights abuses in Saudi Arabia and other countries.*

Index

abortion, 81
absolute monarchy, 7, 10, 12, 34–37
   See also Saud Dynasty
abuses, 13–14, 22–23, 25, 27–28, 40–41, 80–81
Afro-Asians, 85, 89, 91
age distribution, 85–88
agriculture, 6, 59–60, 68
Al Yamamah Palace, 48
alcohol, 42
alliances, 20, 23–26
al-Qaeda, 19, 26–27
Al-Ula, 10
anti-Americanism, 20–22
Arabian Peninsula, 7, 26
Arabic (language), 85, 90
Arab-Israeli War (1973), 8–9
Arabs, 85, 89
arrests, 36, 79–81
   See also religious authorities
atheism, 36
automobiles, 12, 61, 73–74, 81
Ayatollah Khomeini, 32

Badawi Najdi (language), 90
Bahrain, 8
banking, 52–55
Basic Law, 45
   See also constitution
Berber (language), 91
Buddhism, 36, 88
burqa, 11

Canada, 22
censorship, 77–78
   See also religious authorities
Central Najdi (language), 90–91
children, 27–28, 72–73
China, 24, 26
Christianity, 36, 47, 77, 88
clerics, 7, 11, 14, 20, 26
climate, 6, 86
Cold War, 23–24
commercial law, 47–48
conflicts, 8–9, 16, 18, 22–27, 30–31, 80, 106
   See also religion
Confucianism, 36
constitution, 34–35, 43, 45
   See also Basic Law
Consultative Assembly, 34, 48–49
corruption, 14, 17, 39, 68
courts, 43, 46–48, 50–51
   See also legal system
crackdowns, 25, 39–40
criminal law, 46–47
criminality, 73

culture, 11, 43–44, 49, 84–98
currency, 52–55

Dammam, 6
dates, 59–60, 92
death penalty, 19, 25, 29, 33
   See also executions
defense, 22, 29–30
demographics, 6, 55, 66–91
desalination, 52, 62, 70, 72
   See also water
desert reclamation, 68
dialects, 84, 90–91
diet, 59, 92–95
discrimination, 13, 84–85, 88–89
diseases, 67
dissent, 13–14
divorce, 47, 59
Dubai, 59

economy, 40, 42, 52–64
   See also investments; Saudi Vision 2030
edicts, 7, 12
education, 11–12, 42, 55, 74–76, 78, 81, 83
Egypt, 25, 50
Eid al-Adha, 95–96, 98
Eid al-Fitr, 95–96, 98
elections, 35, 43, 48
electricity, 62, 67
embargoes, 7–9
   See also oil embargo (1973)
energy, 52, 61–64
environment, 78, 86
ethnic groups, 85, 89
executions, 40–41, 46, 49
executive branch, 34
exports, 53, 59–61
extremism, 18–21, 30–31, 33–34, 43, 66, 68, 81

family law, 47
fertility rate, 67, 86
foods, 59–61, 92–95
foreign relations, 18, 20–22, 25–26
foreigners, 19, 27–29, 55–59, 70–73, 78–79,
   89–92
France, 16, 33, 80
freedoms, 11–12, 81
   See also rights

geography, 6–8
government, 34–50, 68, 88–89
Grand Mosque, 16, 32–33, 98, 106
Grand Mufti, 32
Great Mosque, 13
gross domestic product (GDP), 53

Gulf Arabic (language), 90–91
Gulf War, 30, 78

Hajj, 13, 54, 91, 105
   See also pilgrims
health care, 55, 67, 70, 73–74, 78
health insurance, 70, 78
Hejazi (language), 90
Hinduism, 36
history, 6–9, 38, 43–44, 54, 87–91, 105
holidays, 35, 43–44, 95–98
homosexuality, 81
House of Saud, 8
housing, 58–59, 72, 74
Houthis, 18, 22–23
human rights, 12–13, 22–25, 27–28, 39–41, 81
Human Rights Watch, 23, 81–82
human trafficking, 27–28, 73

Ikhwan, 32
illegal drugs, 19, 29
immigration, 84
imports, 53, 55, 60–61, 75
independence, 35
   See also National Day
industry, 53
inequality, 48, 58, 74, 91
   See also women
infrastructure, 14, 42, 68, 70, 75, 84
International Institute for Strategic Studies, 29
Internet access, 67, 75–77
investments, 36–37, 42, 47–48, 50, 59
Iran, 18, 22–23, 25, 27, 30, 32, 89
Iraq, 8, 30–31
Islam, 8, 11, 14, 16, 47, 85
Islamic State of Iraq and al-Sham (ISIS), 19, 26–27, 77
Israel, 8–9, 26, 77

Jeddah, 6, 62
Jordan, 8
journalism, 13–14, 58, 67, 79–80
Judaism, 47, 77, 82
judges, 43, 46–49
   See also legal system
judicial branch, 50–51
   See also courts; judges; legal system

Kabba, 13
Kerry, John, 35
Khan, Sabica, 13
Khashoggi, Jamal, 13–14, 17, 80
kidnapping, 73
king. *See* monarch
King Saud University, 82
Kingdom of Hejaz, 54, 70, 105
Kuwait, 8, 30–31

labor force, 53, 55–56, 75, 78–79
languages, 84–85, 90–92

law enforcement, 36
   See also mutaween; religious authorities
legal system, 19, 35, 42–43, 45–48, 50, 68, 79
   See also courts; judges; Sharia Law
legislature, 34, 48–49
LGBTQ, 50, 81
life expectancy, 67, 78, 88
literacy, 67

Mahdi, 32
   See also Twelfth Imam
majils. See Consultative Assembly
malnutrition, 66, 68
marriage, 47
Masmak Fortress, 6, 38
MbS. *See* Salman, Mohammed bin (crown prince)
Mecca, 6, 13, 16, 58, 90, 105
media, 67, 84
medicine, 42, 61, 70, 74, 78
Medina, 6, 56, 105
MeToo movement, 13
Middle East tensions, 25–27, 30–32
military, 7, 18–19, 22–23, 29–30
Ministry of Health, 70
Modern Standard Arabic, 90
modernization, 12–13, 40, 75–77, 84–88
mortality rate, 67, 73, 86
Muhammad (prophet), 11, 13, 18, 96, 105
murder, 13, 46, 73
Muslim Brotherhood, 26
mutaween, 84, 88
   See also religious authorities

Najdi (language), 90
National Day, 35–36, 43, 95, 97
national identification cards, 43, 79
natural resources, 6, 8, 40, 52, 59–64
Nichols, Jason, 91
Nimr, Nimr al- (sheikh), 41
nomadic tribes, 8, 74, 84, 87, 90
Non-Aligned Movement, 23–24
nutrition, 59–61, 66, 68, 92–95

oil, 8, 40, 52, 55, 59–63, 78
oil embargo (1973), 7–9, 26, 88, 106
opposition, 34, 36, 40–41, 80
   See also arrests
Organization of Petroleum Exporting Countries (OPEC), 26, 88

passports, 28, 73
per capita income (PPP), 53, 68
Persian Gulf, 6, 8, 26, 82, 90
personal information, 79
petroleum, 8, 40, 52, 59–61, 63–64, 78
pilgrims, 13, 54, 71
   See also Hajj
political parties, 48–50
politics, 34–40, 42–50, 68, 88–89

polygamy, 47
population, 6, 55, 60, 67–72, 85
poverty, 58, 91
prime minister, 34
prohibitions, 11, 49, 81
  See also mutaween; religious authorities
protests, 13–14, 24
punishments, 46, 49, 73, 81

Qahtani, Mohammed Abdullah al-, 32
Qassim, 81
Qatar, 8, 26–27, 88
QR Video
  arrests in Saudi Arabia, 79
  crackdown on clerics, 24
  first king of Saudi Arabia, 45
  the Hajj, 98
  tourism, 56
  women's rights, 11
Qu'ran, 32, 43, 45, 49, 82, 85, 96

Ramadan, 95–96, 98
rape, 73
recent news, 17
Red Sea, 6, 8
reforms, 11–12, 37, 40, 44, 48–49
  See also modernization; social changes
religion, 7, 11–16, 18, 20, 25, 30, 32, 36, 44, 82,
  85, 88
  See also conflicts; culture; Islam; Wahhabism
religious authorities, 36, 42, 77, 84, 98
  See also mutaween
rights, 11–13, 43, 47, 79, 81
  See also freedoms
Ritz-Carlton (Riyadh), 25, 39–40
Riyadh, 6, 52, 90
riyal, 52–54
Rohingya (language), 91–92

safety, 73
Salman, Mohammed bin (crown prince), 13–14,
  37–40, 55, 77, 80, 106
sanitation, 42, 68, 70
satellites, 75
Saud, Abdulaziz bin Abdul Rahman Faisal al-
  (founding monarch), 6, 43–44, 50
Saud, Abdullah bin Abdulaziz al- (monarch), 43
Saud, Faisal bin Abdulaziz al- (monarch), 43
Saud, Salman bin Abdulaziz-al (monarch), 10,
  13, 25, 34–35
Saud, Saud bin Abdulaziz al- (monarch), 44
Saud Dynasty, 6–8, 10–11, 34–43, 48–50, 105–106
  See also history
Saudi Vision 2030, 42, 55, 78
Saudi-Yemeni conflict, 17–18, 22–23, 26, 80, 106
security forces, 13–14, 80
September 11, 2001, 20–21
sex ratio, 85, 87–88
sexual harassment, 13, 28
Sharia Law, 35, 45–49, 79

See also legal system
Shi'a Islam, 8, 11, 18, 20, 22, 90
slavery, 28, 89, 91
social changes, 11–16, 36, 42, 55, 74, 82–84
  See also reforms
social media, 13, 47, 77–78, 81
society, 84–98
socioeconomic mobility, 78
solar energy, 52, 62–63
special tribunals, 48
spending, 18–19, 22, 29–30
sports, 7, 87
subsidies, 52, 55, 63–64, 66, 68, 70, 74–75
Sunna, 45–46, 49
Sunni Islam, 8, 11, 18, 22
  See also culture; Wahhabism
Syria, 25, 27

Tagalog (language), 91–92
Taoism, 36
tawaf, 13
technology, 42, 59
telecommunications, 67
terrorism, 18–21, 26–27, 30–33, 46
tobacco, 61
tolerance, 36, 81
totalitarianism, 34–36
tourism, 8, 10, 14, 40, 42, 56
trade, 22–25, 53, 59–61
transgenders, 81
Trump, Donald, 27, 80
Turkey, 80
Twelfth Imam, 16, 32, 106

ulema, 45–46
unemployment, 53, 73
United Arab Emirates (UAE), 8, 25, 59, 88
United Kingdom (UK), 24, 80
United Nations (UN), 17, 26, 73, 78
United States (US), 8, 10, 20, 23–24, 26, 29–30,
  59, 80
  See also US military bases
universities, 11, 75–76, 82–83
urban centers, 6, 13, 16, 56, 58, 62, 86, 90
Urdu (language), 91–92
US military bases, 26–27, 30

voting, 11, 35, 43

Wahhabism, 8, 11–12, 14, 22, 44, 81–82, 88–89
  See also mutaween; religious authorities
wars, 8, 18, 22–24, 26, 30–31, 78, 80, 106
water, 52, 62, 70–72
Western fashion, 36, 61, 77–78
wind energy, 52, 63
women, 11–13, 22, 27–28, 36, 43–44, 47–48, 59,
  73, 77–78, 81–87

Yemen, 6, 8, 18, 22–24, 26
youth, 66, 73, 84, 87–88

Author's Biography

Norm Geddis lives in Southern California, where he works as a writer, video editor, and collectibles expert. He once spent two years cataloging and appraising over 1 million old movie props. Previous books for Mason Crest include the World of Automobiles series. He is currently restoring the film and video content from the 1950s DuMont Television Network for the Days of DuMont channel on Roku.

Credits

Cover

Interior